Harriet Shaw

Recent books by
Mignon G. Eberhart

Jury of One
The Cup, the Blade or the Gun
Enemy in the House
Run Scared
Call After Midnight
R.S.V.P. Murder
Witness at Large
Woman on the Roof

Woman on the roof

Mignon G. Eberhart

Woman on the roof

RANDOM HOUSE *New York*

First Printing

LIBRARY OF CONGRESS CATALOG CARD NUMBER: 67–22626

Manufactured in the United States of America
by The Haddon Craftsmen, Inc., Scranton, Pennsylvania

Designed by Stephanie Tevonian

All persons and events in
this book are completely imaginary.

Woman on the roof

chapter 1

There were times when the shadow on the terrace seemed to take on the shape of a woman's body flung down, left in its blood and beauty. The snows of five winters and the rains of four summers had washed the smooth red tiles of the terrace floor. The terrace had been scrubbed almost daily during five springs and four summers and four autumns. Even if once in fact there had been a shadow, it would have disappeared.

All the same Susan Desart fancied for a moment again that she saw the shadow of her predecessor, a woman whom she had admired. Nobody could have helped liking Rose Desart, with the shocking exception of the person who had killed her, there in the corner of the terrace, close to the gate opening on the rest of the roof, which had been too securely padlocked to allow Rose to elude her murderer.

The gate adjoined the entrance to the fire escape, which was shielded by a long box of privet hedge. It was possible that this very box of privet, a little weather-beaten by rain and snow and winter winds, cast a shadow. But the April day was cold and overcast, with rain threatening, so there could be no shadow, no shadow at all. She put aside her fancy and kneeled down to dig into one of the porch boxes which stood below the great windows of the penthouse where she lived with her husband, Marcus Desart. Flats which held little pots of salmon-colored geraniums and glossy green ivy stood helter-skelter on the terrace.

The awnings were not yet up; the terrace furniture had not yet been brought up from the storeroom twelve stories down. But she had ordered the plants that morning; they had been instantly delivered and now must be removed from their little pots and planted in the porch boxes. With her trowel she dug down, loosened some soil, crumbled it in her gloved fingers and gently placed the first geranium. As she arranged it carefully in the box so that its roots had space, a man spoke from the door into the house.

"Hello, Sue."

Her father had called her Susan; everyone else called her Sue. She sat back to look, and a man came out, wended his way through the scattered flats and stood smiling down at her. His hair was crisp black, his eyes blue and laughing, his features rather blunt and solid; he was very good to look at. She smiled, because nobody could help responding to Douglas Woodard's cheerful grin. "Woody! I didn't hear you come."

"I rang downstairs. Pauline let me in. Who's the new elevator man?"

"I don't know his name yet. He's been here only a day or two."

"What happened to old Groves?"

"He had to leave. Arthritis, poor old fellow. He worked here thirty years." She patted the loose soil carefully around the geranium with its brave bright blossoms as a big raindrop splashed down beside her.

Woody said suddenly, with surprise, "You're using the same terrace flowers Rose always used."

"Yes. It was in her day book." She looked up at the gray sky and a drop fell on her face.

"Her what?"

Sue surveyed the flats of geraniums and ivy. A little rain would probably be good for them. "Marcus found it for me last night. He said she called it her day book. I can't make out much of it. It's a sort of housekeeping book, order book, recipes, menus, that kind of thing. The first week of April said, 'Florist order terrace,' and there was a phone number." She got up from her kneeling position. "One geranium planted. It isn't much."

"Did you remember that she always used bright pink geraniums and ivy?"

"No, I didn't. The florist knew. The moment I said that I was Mrs. Marcus Desart and wanted to talk to him about the terrace flowers for the summer, he said he had the right color geraniums and the ivy. He'd ordered, thinking I would want the same thing the first Mrs. Desart always used. So of course I said yes and he had them delivered. It's going to pour, Woody. Let's go in. Marcus should come home soon."

"I'd far rather talk to you than to Marcus, darling."

His voice was teasing. She laughed. "Now that's a nice compliment." She gathered up trowel and fork and removed her loose gloves.

"Oh now, Sue, how do you know that I don't mean it!" There was an unexpected shade of seriousness in his voice.

She glanced at him in surprise. His face was sober and he was looking thoughtfully around the terrace.

She said, "Those willows took a beating this winter, but I think they'll perk up."

A few green tubs of willows were grouped around the terrace; later, when the furniture had been brought up and the awnings returned from storage and put up, the tubs would be more carefully arranged. Spring had been slow in coming. The privet hedges still looked bare; the budding leaves gave as yet only a tinge of green. Though the willows had begun their spring emergence into yellow, they were only a haze of slender branches that drooped disconsolately.

"It's the north wind," Woody said. "West wind, too. It's hard to make trees grow."

"That willow on the end is really sick. I think it ought to be tied up to the awning support, there on the northwest corner perhaps."

"Want me to do it now?"

"I'll have to get a ladder."

"Oh, I can stand on the terrace balustrade and reach over."

A red brick and concrete parapet ran along the outer length and far end of the terrace; the other two sides were enclosed by the walls of the penthouse itself, except for the gate to the roof. The parapet was perhaps three feet high and there was a flat concrete top to it about a foot wide.

She cried, "Woody! You do realize it's twelve stories down!"

"Have you got anything to tie it with? There used to be garden stuff in a chest in the gallery."

"Now, listen—oh, here comes the rain."

It came in a rush, helter-skelter, upon them, upon the bright geraniums, upon the young ivy plants, upon the red-tiled terrace, and upon the shadow that was not there. They ran for the door into the penthouse, and Woody pushed Sue through first. She caught her breath and put down her gardening gloves and trowel and fork. "I've got to see about the windows. Sit down, I'll be back—"

She hurried through the gallery and the living room and on into her bedroom, which was on the northwest corner and took the onslaught of rains and winds harder than any other portion of the penthouse. She closed two windows, ran into the dressing room, closed two more there, and then those in Marcus' room which faced east. She went back through the dressing room, pausing at a big mirror to comb back her hair, which the rain and wind had tousled. Owing to the swift dusk brought by the storm, her face in the mirror looked white, and her red-brown hair had lost its shine. She brushed at her green tweed skirt where she had been kneeling on the terrace, and shoved up the sleeves of her green sweater. The ring Marcus had given her flashed dully in the semi-gloom.

She went back through her bedroom and directly into the long living room. It was a beautiful room; as always, she paused for a second, looking at the soft grays and yellows, the dramatic sweep of green curtains which could be drawn across the great windows on either side of the fireplace. The mantel was of pale yellow marble, gracefully carved. The long sofa was a muted yellow too; there were graceful armchairs and delicate tables. Along one wall a Chippendale wall desk stood, its glass-paneled doors aglitter. A huge bowl of massed white lilacs on a low table set up a sweet fragrance. Every lamp, every crystal or silver ashtray, every small bit of porcelain, even the little French clock on the mantel, its enameled pendulum swinging briskly back and forth behind glass walls, had been selected by Rose. Marcus' big chair was covered in green too, and Sue admired

Rose's unerring taste; the room looked as if it had grown just like this, in utter harmony but without plan.

Woody had turned on the lamp on the big table by a window and was bending over Rose's day book, which lay on the table. The room had a pleasantly soft glow; rain beat hard, slanting down the long windowpanes. Woody said, "Is this the day book?"

It was a very practical book, merely a black looseleaf notebook, over half filled with Rose's vigorous handwriting. It was, however, almost too economic a handwriting; apparently Rose had evolved her own kind of shorthand, for there were initials, figures, phone numbers and addresses without names, which would have made reading a puzzle to anyone but the writer. Rose's menus, however, were written out clearly, and Marcus had said they would be a help to Sue if or when they began to have dinner parties. There were guest lists that were sometimes fully written out and sometimes merely initials. Apparently some of the people listed had allergies, and Rose had carefully made a note of these; she had also noted the kinds of food and cigarettes frequent guests liked and sometimes the cocktails or wine. Rose had been efficient.

"That's it," Sue said.

Woody idly turned over a leaf. "Initials. Very cryptic notes, I must say."

"Of course, she knew what they meant. She was so lovely, so—oh, charming. And so capable."

Woody flipped over some of the pages with their neat black notations. "You liked her."

"Who could help liking her? It was a senseless, horrible thing."

Woody paused. "Why, this is the last entry."

"Yes, I saw it. That is, I saw the date, August twelfth. It's only some directions to Pauline—at least, I saw Pauline's name and some notes. I didn't read them. I couldn't understand her notes, anyway. She abbreviated everything. But that last day—no, I didn't want to read what she had written."

Woody leaned over, the light from the table full upon his good-looking, sober face; his black eyelashes made rims of shadow on his cheekbones. "Poor Rose. Her last day. Looks as if she broke off, whatever it was. I wonder why she stopped."

"Oh, something happened, the telephone or—"

"Or someone came," Woody said and then seemed to realize what he had said, for he closed the book abruptly. It was too clear that the person who might have interrupted Rose's entry could have been her murderer.

Sue put her hand upon the book. "I'd better put it away."

Woody looked out at the terrace where now rain was beating hard upon the flowers, the pots of ivy and the shadow that did not exist at the corner of the terrace. "Did the police ever see that book?"

"The police! I shouldn't think so. Marcus got it from the kitchen, I think." But because it had belonged to Rose she felt that she ought to take care of it. She picked it up.

Woody said, "Oh, well, it's not important. But I do wish that the police had managed to nail the murderer and get him convicted. Poor old Marcus. He's got to get over his notion that people always will suspect him. You know, elderly man married to a young and beautiful woman. I suppose he thinks of that damnable old thing people will always say—no smoke without fire."

Sue said sharply, "There's the elevator. Marcus is coming."

She had an obscure feeling that it might hurt Marcus to see Rose's day book and to guess that she and Woody had been talking of it and his dead wife. The private elevator, which Marcus himself had had installed years before when he had bought the penthouse, hummed nearer. She took the book and crossed the long room again to her bedroom. There was a graceful chest of drawers, French, with a pleasant bowed front, just inside the room. She thrust the black notebook into a drawer, down among some stockings, and returned to the living room as the hum of the elevator stopped.

A door, paneled with wood, swung open, and Marcus pushed back the elevator grille and came into the room. A smile for Sue was already fixed upon his face. His eyes brightened when he saw Woody, too. He wore a raincoat; the shoulders were wet. His hair was dark and vigorous, barely touched with silver on top like a crest. He had strongly marked features; in his youth he must have been an extremely handsome man. Sue could remember him from her childhood, though rather vaguely, only as a smiling friend of her father's who occasionally took her on his knee and talked to her. She recalled him more clearly from her adolescence, when she was old enough to come to the penthouse with her father for an occasional cocktail party. But she remembered him most clearly at the time of her father's illness and death, when Marcus, whenever he was in the city, had turned up early and late, sitting with the sick man, bringing him a surreptitious bottle of whiskey or box of cigars; her father was supposed to have neither, but both he and Marcus knew that it really didn't matter. And then Marcus had found her a job in a friend's office, and he had telephoned her occasionally to see how she was getting along. Rose had kept in touch with her, too, although less frequently. Marcus had helped her sell the big apartment in this same building on the sixth floor which her father had owned and where Sue had spent most of her life, and had advised her about investing the money. Last winter

Marcus had asked her to marry him. Both of them knew why. There had been no secret, no misunderstanding; it had all been clear, and their marriage had been successful for exactly what it was.

Sue hurried over to him now and put up her face for his kiss. His face was wet and cool with rain. He lifted his head, shrugged out of his raincoat and laughed. "It poured for a few minutes. I got all this just coming from the corner. I had the taxi leave me at the cross street rather than go around the block. Good to see you, Woody."

Sue took the raincoat, shook it and crossed to the long gallery, which was like a hall between the living room and stairs. It was lined on the terrace side by a continuing row of windows that lined and lighted the living room. At the end of the gallery a spiral stairway twisted down to the first floor of the penthouse. Of course, this was only Marcus' New York home; she had never seen his house in his native state. In fact, since most of Marcus' law practice was carried on in his office here, he himself remained for most of the year in what he called his "New York roost." It was an elegant roost.

Like many penthouses, the apartment was an afterthought of the architects of the big and luxurious apartment building; consequently it had odd angles and ingenious, sometimes inconvenient, arrangements. Sue went down the stairway to a small foyer, where there was a coat closet, and hung up Marcus' coat. From this small foyer a door led to another, public, hall which did not belong to the penthouse but was used by two other apartment owners on the eleventh floor. Here too were doors to the elevator which served the entire apartment house, and this was the customary approach of guests and visitors. Only she, Marcus and Pauline had keys to the door for the private elevator, which was inconspicuous and directly beside the main elevator shaft in the main lobby. Sue rarely used her key and the private elevator, for she preferred the big elevator which was serviced by a man, day and night, and never quite trusted herself to the small private cage with its own machinery, which Marcus must have had installed at ruinous cost.

On this floor, the eleventh, the apartment was not, strictly speaking, a penthouse; the entire floor had once been a single apartment. When the floor on the roof, the twelfth, had been built, this apartment had been changed into the first floor of what the deeds referred to as a duplex penthouse.

The small foyer led also into a large dining room. A kitchen, pantry, two maids' rooms and a bathroom were behind the dining room; beyond it on the west there was a small study and lounge.

Sue strolled over to the window. It was possible that Woody had come to talk to Marcus of politics. She hoped that her husband might sometime be induced to again take an active interest; politics and his wife Rose had once been the mainsprings of his life.

She looked out over rooftops and little gusts of black smoke. A gull wheeled past, looking rather cross and casting a rapacious eye downward.

chapter 2

The rain had stopped as suddenly as it had begun, but the sky was still a leaden gray. One of the smokestacks nearby began to belch black smoke; it would continue for about five minutes and then vanish, but that would be enough to send a fine drift of soot across the terrace and in through any open windows. It was one of the penalties, Sue had already discovered, of living in a penthouse. But there were rewards too; across Madison and Fifth avenues she could see the thin young greens of Central Park. Later, from the living room and terrace upstairs, she would see the fabled, lighted towers of Manhattan shining against the sky. Sometimes, early in the morning, she could hear a faint shrill piping from some Navy ship anchored in the river; she always tried to shut her ears to that.

A thin, bright green line floated lazily downward directly before her eyes. She stared at it in bewilderment as it drifted down out of sight, but she recognized it. It was a piece of the soft green twine used for tying up the top-heavy shrubbery. Or for tying up a willow tree, she thought swiftly; Woody was tying up the willow tree. But he didn't have a ladder—the only one was kept in a closet off the kitchen. He wouldn't be such a fool as to climb up on the parapet!

But with the thought, she ran across the dining room and up the stairs. At the top she saw Woody himself plunging through the living room. She ran for the door to the terrace, but he thrust her aside so hard that she fell on a bench. As he ran on, over his shoulder she saw a terrifying tableau.

Marcus was standing on the parapet, leaning over the privet hedge with its tiny green leaves, reaching for the drooping willow and the awning support. Apparently he had dropped the piece of twine which she had seen floating lazily downward, but he had another in one hand. His slender figure, his head, his gray coat and neatly striped tie were all part of a picture frozen in time. As she watched, he looked down and down, wavered and put his hand to his head. Then Woody seized him, and the two men grappled and fell to the floor of the terrace, where they both struggled for balance before getting up.

As they separated, Sue sank back on the bench; her knees wouldn't hold her up.

Marcus rubbed his eyes and grinned feebly at Woody. Woody shrugged his coat into place and put his hand under Marcus' elbow. "Okay now?"

"Good God," said Marcus, then saw Sue. "I'm sorry—"

"Come on," Woody said. "Let's go in."

They passed through the gallery, Woody's hand still

under Marcus' arm, and went into the living room. Sue, still shaken, followed them slowly.

Marcus collapsed into his big armchair. Woody said feelingly, "I'd like a drink!"

Marcus took a long breath. "We could all do with a drink. I'm sorry you saw that, Sue."

"Marcus." She couldn't say another word.

Woody went over to the bar built into the beautiful Chippendale wall desk. He let down its leaf, and bottles and glasses and decanters glittered. Sue reached for a switch and turned on all the lights; the room sprang into color and loveliness, as if nothing at all had happened. The fragrance from the white lilacs was sweet and tranquil.

Nothing *has* happened, Sue thought, but she went to Marcus' chair and sat on the arm. He was still breathing heavily. Woody splashed whiskey into a glass. "Oh, I didn't think about ice," Sue said, rising quickly and going to the elevator. Marcus said something about nobody wanting ice, but she pressed the button to open the door to bring the elevator up to the living room. Pauline, ever practical and hating the spiral stairway, used a small table in it as a dumbwaiter. Sue heard the hum as the elevator shook a little and started upward. When it stopped she opened the door and took the tray bearing ice, a silver pitcher of water and a small dish of lemon peel.

Woody thanked her and took the tray. "Whiskey for you?" he asked. "Or a spot of brandy?"

"I don't care. Anything." She sat down on a footstool near Marcus, who gave her a more natural look and smile. "I was a great fool," he said apologetically. "It looked so simple. I've done it before. There's always been trouble with the trees on the terrace; the wind and storms seem to hit the spot broadside. I've often tied the willows up."

"Just don't do it again." Her throat still felt stiff and tight.

Woody put a glass in her hand. "Drink it down. It's a good slug of brandy." He smiled, but he still looked a little white and shaken.

Marcus reached over to put his hand over Sue's. "Really, I'm ashamed. I gave you a fright, I realize. But I've done it before, except"—he glanced wryly at Woody—"perhaps I never looked down before. Well, never mind. I promise you, Sue, I'll never do such a fool thing again. Woody, I rather think you saved my life."

"That was luck." Woody sat down and took a long swallow from the glass in his hand. "I was coming from the phone. I looked out on the terrace and just happened to see you balancing out there on the parapet. It looked . . . Well, it's over." He drank again, sighed and said, "Is this a good time to ask a favor of you, Marcus?"

Sue could almost feel her husband stiffen, as if he guessed what was coming. He smiled, though, and shrugged. "I couldn't think of a better time. But no politics. I'm through with that forever—"

Woody broke in. "Please, Marcus. It's only a small dinner. Only your good friends—"

"From home? What is all this, Woody? No, wait—I can guess. You've got some leading men from my home state here and they're going to try to talk me into running for office. Am I right?"

"Well . . . yes."

Marcus said after a moment, "This must have been planned for some time."

"I—yes, I suppose they've been thinking of it. Writing letters to key people and all that. They came here yesterday and today. They want to talk to you personally, of course."

"And they delegated you to get me to meet them and talk to them."

"Naturally, nobody can go ahead with any specific plans until they get the green light from you."

Marcus smiled thinly. "It would have been far easier and more practical for me to go home and see them, wouldn't it?"

"They knew you wouldn't," Woody said frankly. "There are only a few of them, but they're important, Marcus. They want you back in politics, and this time the chances are good for your getting elected—"

"No," Marcus said. "Any political ambition, any interest I had in running for any office is gone. Never again."

Woody leaned forward. "Listen, Marcus. It's been almost six years since . . . since that happened. It'll be six years in August. Nobody ever blamed you in the first place. It was only your absurd—I mean"—Woody caught himself—"your sensitive notion of honor that made you decide to step out of politics. But by now— No, hear me out," he said, for Marcus had lifted his hand to stop him. "Listen to me just this one time. Nobody blamed you—how could they? Nobody ever speculated and passed on rumors, as you thought they would. Everybody knows you and your integrity. They want to vote for you, and election year is coming up."

Marcus said quietly, "The answer is still no."

Sue was surprised to hear herself say, "Marcus, consider it. Won't you?"

He looked at her, his dark eyebrows drawn sternly over his blazing gray eyes. "Why, Sue!"

She felt Woody's approval, but he sat very still, holding his glass.

Perhaps the brandy and the letdown from that instant of terror had given her courage. She said, "Marcus, this is important to you. I think Woody is right. It's your decision, of course, but how can it hurt anything or anybody simply to talk to these men who have come all the way to see you? Most of them must be old friends."

Marcus smiled absently, then rose and walked across to the windows. He stood there, his back turned to the room. She guessed that he didn't want either of them to see how moved he was.

Woody had the wisdom not to speak. Together they watched the spare but erect shoulders outlined against the window and the darkening sky beyond the terrace. For an odd instant an unpleasant thought touched Sue; she hoped that her husband was not seeing a certain shadow in the corner of the terrace which could not possibly be there.

Suddenly Marcus turned around to face them. His fine head was lifted, and his voice had its old natural resonance. He had an orator's voice, an actor's way of moving; it was nothing assumed; it was natural to him; it had been a great gift, as a matter of fact, in his political career. "All right, Sue. All right, Woody. I'll go. I'll not deny that it will give me some pleasure. But I'll never run for any office—that's in the past. You understand that, Woody."

"Of course." Woody was too smart, too fully a product of Marcus' teaching to show even by the flicker of an eyelash, by the slightest jauntiness in his manner, that he had achieved a triumph. He said, "The dinner is early. Perhaps we'd better start soon. Several of them plan to get the night plane home."

"I'll wash up," Marcus said briefly. He went into his bedroom, moving like a young man.

Sue looked at Woody, who gave her a conspiratorial wink and then finished his drink thoughtfully. Presently Marcus came back. Sue's heart gave a little twitch like pity, except it wasn't pity, when she saw that he had swiftly changed into a new suit. He looked young and spruce and capable. He had chosen his tie carefully too, and wore a fresh white shirt. He looked like the distinguished Marcus Desart who was trusted and admired and honored, and who might have held public office if his wife Rose Desart had not been murdered.

Sue's voice was a little unsteady. She said, "Have a good time," which was so ordinary that Marcus seemed to understand she didn't know how to say what she meant.

He lifted her chin. "Thank you, my dear. I'll be home early."

Woody gave her another look, which clearly said, "I'll do my best to get him to listen." But his only words were, "Goodnight, Sue."

They went into the little elevator; the door closed and it murmured downward. When Sue could no longer hear it, she gathered up the empty glasses and replaced them on the tray. The terrace doors in the gallery were still open; the air was pleasantly cool and moist after the rain. The sky was a darkening blue and a few stars were shining. The lights from the gallery and living-room windows fell upon the salmon-pink geraniums. There was no shadow at all on the terrace; there had never been a shadow, and now beyond the lights from the windows everything was dark. She closed the door, locking it and attaching the chain bolt which Marcus had had installed. Quietly but seriously, he had told her never to leave any of the doors to the penthouse unlocked; nor was she ever to answer the doorbell unless she knew who stood outside. He hadn't needed to explain it.

Taking the tray downstairs, she told Pauline, who was busy in the kitchen, that Mr. Desart would not be in to dinner, and that she would have dinner on a tray in the study. This suited Pauline. "If Madame will—there is the cinema—" What she actually said was, "Zere is ze cinema—" She would have spoken in French if her mistress had understood it; as it was, Sue caught about one word in ten of Pauline's savage staccato attack upon her native tongue.

Sue nodded her permission, then went back upstairs and sat in Marcus' green armchair. She thought about Marcus and about Rose Desart; then, because when she was alone he came into her thoughts and heart and her whole being, as if he were still alive, she thought about Jim Locke. After a while she went to her bedroom. In the drawer below her stocking drawer there lay a small, shabby candy box, tied with a string. In it were all the things she had left of Jim.

chapter 3

Sue was tempted to take out the box and open it, but did not. She knew its contents. There were some letters, one or two cables, the final telegram, not from the War Office, naturally, but from his mother. There were some tiny objects which meant nothing to anybody else, such as an empty book of matches from a restaurant in the Fifties. She had kept it, foolishly and sentimentally, because she and Jim had dined there so often. In one corner was a small white velvet box, lined in satin; a ring with a modest diamond was wedged in it. She had been engaged to marry Jim Locke. They were going to marry as soon as he had another leave. But then he didn't have a leave. He was a Navy pilot and he had been shot down. He would never return, so she had married Marcus. He had put out his hand to help her; she hoped that she had helped him.

She loved Jim and her memory of him, and she couldn't rid herself of either love or memory. She knew she ought to get rid of the letters and put the diamond ring away somewhere, but the few contents of the box hurt only herself, and then only on the rare occasions when she looked at it, or even opened it and counted over her small treasures. But she wouldn't give up the box yet.

She wouldn't look at it that night, however. She knew she was still shaken by the terrifying instant when Marcus had wavered there on the parapet, twelve stories above the street level. The brandy had helped at the time, but now its effect was wearing off. She shut the drawer and went into the big dressing room between her and Marcus' bedrooms. She turned on the lights, and the charming little room with the ruffled white dressing table, pink bench and mirrors sprang into cheerful being. She wished that she hadn't permitted herself to look at the box of Jim's letters, or to think of him. There must be some way of controlling thoughts, she thought soberly.

Sue washed her face, then brushed her hair and filed a chipped fingernail. She experimented with a new perfume and didn't like it. For something else to do she slid out of her skirt and sweater and into a silk housecoat, short and full, of a vivid green which brought out the red lights in her hair. She must not let herself think of Jim again. It was enough that he was always in the back of her mind, somewhere, seeming to eye her steadily, smiling a little, loving her. No, she would *not* think about that.

She went downstairs slowly. The big dining room was stately with its polished mahogany, its chairs with fine needlepoint seats, the massive silver on the sideboard. The lounge was supposed to be a study for Marcus, but the big desk usually bore only magazines and newspapers and a paper cutter, for he had the politician's habit of clipping everything that interested him or bore upon some subject, usually controversial, which might be coming up before the House or the Senate.

Pauline had heard her mistress crossing the dining room, and entered with a tray. She was already dressed in the chic black of the Frenchwoman, a neat dress, a simple black coat and false but handsome pearls at her throat. Her black hair was smartly puffed out. She rattled out something in quick French and then repeated in perfectly clear English that she wouldn't be late.

"Have you your key?"

"Oh, but yes, madame. Thank you, madame. I'll see to the tray à mon retour."

"M'm—yes. All right."

Pauline frisked out, her high heels tapping on the polished parquet floor of the dining room.

Rose's mother wouldn't like the liberties which Pauline was inclined to take with her daughter's successor. Rose's mother believed in the rules and customs of a domestic service which Sue knew had gone forever.

Pauline had been at "ze cinema" the day Rose was murdered.

Rose had been born in Marcus' native state, and there she and Marcus had met and married. Afterward, when it developed that Marcus would be spending most of his time in New York (and just possibly, if elected, in Washington) Belle Minot, Rose's mother, had followed the two of them to New York. In fact, she lived in an apartment only a few streets away from Marcus' "roost." Sometimes Sue wondered idly about Marcus' real home, which she had never visited. "It's grim," Belle had told her once. "Early nineteen-hundreds, a mint of money spent on it. Marcus will never be able to sell it and you'll never want to live there. He keeps his legal residence there and a sort of token office. But"—Belle smiled—"I'm fully settled here now. I couldn't pull up stakes and move back. I'm a displaced person now, like so many New Yorkers, and I like it."

Sometime Marcus would have to visit his home; certainly he would have to return there and campaign if his friends persuaded him to run for office.

Having finished her dinner, Sue took the tray to the pantry and went on to make sure that the kitchen door was locked. Then she made a little tour of the entire place. The fact was that there were too many ways of getting in and out of the penthouse; this had made the police investigation into Rose's murder harder. There was the kitchen door, which opened upon a back hall and a service elevator. There were the doors to the private elevator in the dining room and in the living room above it. The private elevator door in the lobby, however, locked automatically and could be opened from the outside only with a key. Then there was the door from the small foyer into the hall, which was shared by the two other apartment owners. The apartment house was a cooperative; everybody knew something about everybody else. That very fact had made Rose Desart's senseless and brutal murder a matter of personal concern for every apartment owner in the building.

Sue put the chain bolt on the door into the public foyer; Marcus would probably use the private elevator when he returned. Then she walked slowly up the winding stairs and onto the gallery. The windows were black now and reflected the lights from gallery and living room; she drew the sage-green curtains across them with a swish that sounded very loud in the silence about her. That silence was another reward for putting up with some of the inconveniences of a penthouse; after the rush-hour traffic from Madison and even from Fifth Avenue had died away, the apartment was always quiet. Sometimes at night a fire engine or an ambulance swooped along a cross street, sometimes a jet plane shrieked loudly overhead; otherwise there was no noise.

If anybody wished to count, and there were plenty of people who *had* counted years ago, there were two more ways in and out of the penthouse. In order to make room for the stairs, the wall of the penthouse jutted out at the end of the terrace. Where it ended, a tall gate of wrought iron, between the parapet and the corner of the penthouse, divided the terrace from the rest of the roof. Also in the same corner but at right angles to the gate, there was an entrance to a fire escape which wound its way down along the west wing of apartments. The gate had been locked on the day of Rose Desart's murder, and a box of hedge stood directly across the entrance to the fire escape; the police had concluded that Rose had been trying to escape, had run from the penthouse, had found the gate locked and the entrance to the fire escape blocked, and that her murderer had struck her down on the terrace. At that time of year, August, the privet hedge was thick, and there were heavy vines obscuring the wrought-iron gate. Rose's murderer had been perfectly safe from observation.

The tragic fact was that Rose Desart herself had cut off her escape either by gate or fire escape, for it was against the law to block either of them. But when the fire inspectors had come around, somehow Rose got wind of it; the gate was open, its padlock gone, and the box of privet hedge had been pushed aside.

She had no sense of fright; yet even after nearly six years, the memory of Rose Desart's murder was sometimes too clear. Perhaps everyone in the apartment house, everyone in the neighborhood, remembered it and took precautions about answering doorbells and locking and bolting doors.

Marcus had removed Rose Desart's portrait, but Sue remembered her well. She was a remarkable beauty, tall and slender and always elegant, with her smooth dark hair and smooth white skin. She was always graceful, and though only in her early thirties, always self-possessed. If there was a pride in her bearing, there was also a kindness which might have been studied but certainly seemed natural; she remembered the names of the entire staff of the apartment house, and their children's names and the schools they attended. No one could be found who might have been said to be her enemy.

The police investigation had raked over every person who could by any chance have had access to the penthouse or the terrace: delivery boys, messenger boys; every visitor whom doormen or elevator men remembered. But they could never find anybody who might have entered the penthouse that hot, sunny day in August and come upon Rose Desart so suddenly that she could not reach the telephone or run downstairs and out to the foyer. She had taken blind refuge on the terrace, and there the secret intruder had battered out her lovely life. Pauline, returning from the moving picture, had found her and telephoned Marcus' New York office, the police, and even Rose's mother, before she herself had hysterics.

The penthouse was now locked, bolted and secure. Sue went to her room and got Rose's day book out of the stocking drawer. Bringing it into the living room, she settled down beside a lamp, intending to search for the name of the awning storage company. Instead she began to think about Marcus. She hoped that his friends and the party leaders would induce him to run for office again. He had been in the middle of an active campaign, one that had been almost certain to succeed, when Rose was murdered. Instantly he had withdrawn from the race. Part of the reason was due to shock and grief, but his firm decision to withdraw permanently from any political activity came later.

There had been newspaper headlines; the story of the murder had been a *cause célèbre*. As Woody had said that afternoon, of course there must be some people who suspected Marcus. The police had questioned him, naturally; they had questioned hundreds of people, but the husband was always, Sue knew, the prime suspect until proved innocent. In the end Marcus could be proved neither innocent nor guilty.

He had been in Washington that day, and had chanced to take the train back to New York instead of the shuttle plane. He had taken a taxi from Pennsylvania Station but had run into the heavy six o'clock traffic; he had stopped the taxi driver on Madison, in the Fifties, and walked the remaining few blocks to the apartment house. The police were there when he arrived.

But Marcus could not prove that he had taken the train. The police, on the other hand, could not prove that he had taken a plane, had somehow avoided the doorman (which would not be difficult, since he, Marcus, knew the apartment house and its routines so well), had unlocked the private elevator, had gone up to the penthouse, murdered his wife and as quietly departed, still unseen—only to return openly later. The passenger lists of all planes from

Washington during the day were scrutinized, and though his name did not appear and nobody was found who had seen him on any plane, suspicion remained. There was always the possibility of human error, that Marcus had given a false name, that somehow he had, in fact, arrived in New York some three or four hours before he was met by the police.

No taxi driver had come forward to state that he had taken a man carrying a briefcase from Penn Station to a traffic snarl somewhere on Madison in the Fifties. There were too many passengers, too many men carrying briefcases; it was the rush hour.

The men he had seen in Washington knew only that he had intended to leave about noon; his New York office knew only that he was expected home that afternoon or evening.

So Marcus could be proved neither guilty nor innocent, and it was the lack of either proof that had determined him to remove himself entirely from politics. He had not taken this serious step without time and deep reflection, but when he did, a hurried decision of his party leaders had induced Penworth Stidger to run instead. Stidger had been elected, and gradually most of Marcus' political associates dropped away.

His law partner, Aubrey Gould, remained a close friend, but that was to be expected. Woody came often to the penthouse, but that was also to be expected, for Woody was a protégé; he had gone straight from law school into Marcus' law office. When Marcus had decided to run for the Senate, Woody had started his own practice; he had been sure that his mentor's campaign would be successful. Marcus and Aubrey Gould had clients to spare; much of the overflow went to Woody, and he had prospered moderately. He obviously felt that he had never repaid the debt of gratitude he owed the older man.

Sue understood that gratitude. One evening Marcus had chanced to meet her in the big lobby of the apartment house after Jim's death. Sometime later, on an impulse, he told Sue, he had invited her to dinner. Two months later they were married, yet not too soon and not without consideration. Marcus' sense of justice impelled him to put arguments against their marriage. She was young; in the nature of things she would meet other, younger men; it was natural that time would lessen or at least dim the grief she felt for Jim Locke.

On the other hand, Marcus said frankly, he could offer her financial security. And he could and did offer a great deal more, for his brilliant mind opened new vistas and his kindness was without flaw; he had enriched her life, and in such a way that she could and did still love the memory of Jim.

Now she flipped absently over a page or two of the day book and was caught by a few phrases in French. These were as abbreviated into Rose's special kind of shorthand as her English was. "Ph." meant telephone; "P.H." meant penthouse; "Mc" meant Marcus. Sue smiled at one explicit phrase: *Toujours quelque damn chose!* This surprised Sue a little; she had never associated Rose Desart's stately beauty with even a faint sense of humor.

She didn't like looking through the day book, though it was in no sense a private record. The abbreviated notes had to do only with housekeeping. She saw a list of caterers, and had started to read a recipe for crème brûlée when the house telephone in the kitchen buzzed. For a long time after Rose's murder, all callers were announced by the doorman for probably every apartment in the building. Gradually this custom had ceased, unless the visitor was a stranger; an experienced doorman or elevator man seems to know "by the prickle of his thumbs" if a caller is in any way not desirable. But Sue was expecting nobody, and she waited a moment, thinking that the doorman had pushed the wrong button by mistake. The tinny buzz continued, though, repeatedly and rapidly, with a feeling of urgency to it. She went downstairs, took the small receiver and shouted into it—it was always well to shout—"This is Mrs. Desart."

The voice that replied was that of old Polk, who had been the doorman ever since she could remember. Even allowing for the vagaries of the telephone, he seemed madly excited. "Mrs. Desart, I have good news for you! Mrs. Desart—"

"Yes, Polk. Don't shout so. I can't understand you. Slower—"

"Good news! I—" There was a jumble, as if he had tripped over his own words. Then he shouted clearly, "It's good news! It's an old friend!"

Something in his excitement communicated itself to her.

Polk shouted, "You'll want to see him. You mustn't be—" She couldn't hear the next word. Then Polk shouted, "A shock, but a good shock, good news!"

She said, "Who? *Who?*"

"It's Mr. Locke! Jim Locke. Commander Locke. He isn't dead. He's home, he's here!"

She must have said something; she must have hung the little receiver on the hook. The kitchen looked just as usual, shining white and chromium. The breakfast dishes were already set out. She couldn't move. Polk must be playing a joke. But he would never be so cruel! She found that she was holding on to the edge of a table so hard that her fingers hurt. What had Polk really said?

The doorbell rang.

She didn't think that she could move, but in an instant she had flung open the door. Jim stood there, exactly as if he'd merely been away for a few days. He wore a brown suit and a white shirt, and Polk, flushed and grinning, was looking over his shoulder. Jim was thin; he was brown; his hair seemed sun-streaked with threads of gray. His eyes were serious and yet warm and shining deeply. Polk gave him a clap on the shoulder and then returned to his elevator and closed the door.

She must have told Jim to come in, but she was conscious of nothing but the fact that he was alive. In a moment she would have flung herself into his arms, but after waiting a little he put out his hand. She took it in her own, and rejoiced in the fact that it was real; she could feel his flesh and his clasp. After another moment he leaned over and lightly touched her cheek with his lips. That was real too.

But there was a barrier between them. Even then, in that dazzling moment, she knew it existed and so did Jim.

She must have led the way upstairs, must have seated herself and told Jim to sit down. All at once tears were raining down her cheeks. He said at last, "There, Sue. I didn't mean to give you such a shock. But I couldn't see any other way."

She wiped at her eyes with the back of her hand. "Here—" He pulled a handkerchief from the pocket of his coat. His clothes were too big for him, she thought absently. He was so thin.

Jim said, "I should have let you know. I should have written, or something. But I had to see you."

"Yes. Oh, yes."

"I saw my mother yesterday. But of course she knew. They put through a phone call to her weeks ago from the base hospital. She told me about your marriage then. But as soon as I got home . . . I had to see you," he said again.

"Yes." The tears wouldn't stop. He looked at her soberly, then glanced around the room and saw the open bar. He brought her a drink, waited a moment, then went back and poured one for himself. Standing there, he said in a low voice, gravely, almost to himself, "You didn't wait, Sue."

chapter 4

It was not a reproach, only a statement of fact. Jim would never blame her. She said, "I believed you were dead."

His eyes came back to her in the direct, clear gaze which she knew so well. "Of course you believed that. There were times"—a faint smile touched his face—"there were times when I almost believed it myself. No, Sue, you were right not to wait. But"—he looked down into his glass and swirled the liquid around—"I had to see you."

"You said your mother told you about . . . my marriage?"

"Yes, right away. So I've known it all the time I was in the hospital. I was going to call you after I talked to her, but she told me, and so I've had time to think about it.

Stop crying, Sue." He wouldn't look at her. He said roughly, "I can't stand it if you keep on crying."

She began to think more clearly, for she sensed how difficult it was for Jim to control himself. She wiped the tears away with his handkerchief, loving the touch of it because it was Jim's. The tide of love between them was stronger than she could have dreamed; it was an irresistible current, pulling them together. The love she had once felt for him now seemed almost childish, merely romantic. This was different; this had gone through grief and despair and had survived and renewed itself; it was stronger than she was, stronger than Jim.

She knew instinctively that she must control herself as Jim had done. She said, "What happened? Jim, tell me—"

He seemed to relax a little when she spoke in a more natural voice. He took a long breath and met her eyes, but then quickly turned away as if he didn't dare look fully at her for long. But he spoke more naturally too.

"Well, they saw my plane go down in the sea. The rescue outfit came over with a helicopter. I had ejected and the parachute opened all right, but I was unconscious. They couldn't find me. I'd been hit—"

"Oh, Jim!"

"It wasn't bad, a leg wound, it healed all right later, but I was unconscious. Somehow I'd got a concussion. I was conscious long enough to cut the shrouds of the parachute and inflate my life jacket, I remember that. But the rescue outfit had to give up. Next thing I knew it was night and I was in some reeds and water, a kind of swamp right by the sea. The current must have carried me there. My seat pack and my survival kit were gone. Maybe somebody saw me, took what he could, was scared and ran away—it's anybody's guess. I drifted off again. I came to later on, I don't know how much later on. I had sense enough then to realize that I didn't have a dinghy—this is a long story."

"I want to hear everything."

"There's a rubber dinghy in the seat pack, so I didn't have that. I didn't have a balloon or my radio or any way to signal for rescue. Somehow I must have crawled away from the area. After a while a friendly Vietnamese found me. He got me to his village. My leg healed up—they did something for it—but then the concussion—oh, you don't want to hear all this."

"Go on."

"After some time—again I don't know how long—the Viet Cong raided the village. Everybody got out, and they got me out too. This happened several times. I'm still a little hazy about those months. I got malaria, and that didn't help. There'd be periods of fever, you see, when I was delirious. There was no quinine. For quite a long time everything was very mixed up in my mind. Food was scarce. They were very good to me, though. I made some attempts to find a friendly unit. I kept hearing that there were Americans or Australians in the vicinity. By that time I'd picked up a few words of the language. Finally, a Viet Cong unit caught up with us. They marched us off to a kind of camp. Actually—" Here Jim grinned, and Sue thought, he always smiles like that, as if half amused at himself. She had to cling to the arms of her chair to prevent herself from running to him. He said, "Actually, they didn't quite know what to make of me. Luckily their ranking officer wasn't very smart. I don't think he ever realized that I was an American naval officer. Every bit of my identification had vanished; my uniform had gone to rags and I was wearing native clothes. Well, anyway, I finally escaped. We were being transferred from one prison camp to another—walking, of course. Some of us were very weak. I made it into the jungle. Then I wandered around for a while. Jungle, mud, leeches—well, that's in the past. I'd meet natives, and at first they'd be afraid of me—and I'd be afraid of them, as a matter of fact. And then when I was able to talk to them, often as not they'd be confused and send me off in the wrong direction. Finally some Marines picked me up. I'd been presumed dead for a long time."

She hadn't waited long enough; she had married Marcus two months ago. She had only herself to blame. Now, in the midst of her wild joy that Jim was alive, there was the bitter reflection that she might have waited a little longer.

"Good old Marines. Sent me off to base hospital, got quinine into me. Got my identity established. Let my mother know I was alive." He took a long, slow drink. "I'll never forget how clean that bed was. How good the soup was. I had a steak."

"My darling, my darling—" He looked at her swiftly, and she put her hand over her mouth.

He went on, quietly and matter-of-factly, but now there was a light in his eyes. "To make it short, they kept me in the base hospital for some time, then sent me to the San Diego hospital. I talked to my mother several times from there. I had time to think, Sue, and after seeing my mother today, I came here. She didn't want me to come, but I had to."

"Yes," she whispered. "Oh, yes."

He put down his drink; the tiny click of glass on wood sounded loud and somehow significant, as if it marked something of moment. But he said only, in the same quiet and matter-of-fact way, "I tried to phone you late this afternoon from the airport. I lost my nerve, so I came into town. You wouldn't believe it, but it took me three hours to get up my courage to come here. Again I was going to phone you; then I decided that I'd simply come. I expected . . . him to be here too."

She knew that he didn't want to mention Marcus' name. He said, "I didn't know how you felt or . . . or anything. But I knew that you were my girl first."

Sue rose and walked to the windows. She pulled open the soft green curtains, which swished as if the first act of a play were about to begin. She thought, No, it's the second act or the third; the first is all over. She said, over her shoulder, "It's too late, Jim."

There was silence behind her. Then he said, simply, "Why?"

"You know."

There was another silence, longer this time. At last Jim said, "When you turn around and face me and tell me that you love Marcus and that you're happy with him, then I'll leave and you can forget that I ever came back."

Lights shone beyond the parapet and the thin foliage of the hedge. Towers of lights shone across the park. There was too much to say; there was nothing at all to say. She heard herself nevertheless: "If I'd known, if I'd waited—"

"Sue!" There was joy in his voice.

"No, no, Jim!" she cried. "I can't! We can't! Marcus has been good to me. Marcus—"

"Look at me."

She clutched at the curtains for support and then turned to face him. He was still sitting quietly, one leg across the other, a foot swinging. "All right, Sue," he said, but gently this time, "are you in love with Marcus?"

"Jim! There's been no time to think, to realize that you've come back, to—"

"You were my girl first. Are you in love with him?"

"Well—no, not as you mean it."

"Not as we were in love?"

"I'm married to Marcus. And besides . . . you must remember Rose Desart's murder."

"Of course. It was in all the papers."

"You remember that Marcus withdrew from politics?"

"Vaguely. What has that to do with us?"

"I'm his wife now—"

"Sue, there's a time in life when nothing but honesty serves. Is he in love with you?"

"Not as you mean it. No."

"Why not?"

"Because of Rose, of course. He loved her. He couldn't ever love anybody else the way he loved Rose. I'm sure of that."

"For God's sake, did he tell you that?"

"He didn't have to tell me. I knew. Just the way he knew that I—"

Jim rose. "Go on."

"He knew that I loved you. He knew that I felt as if everything in the world had gone when you . . . when they said you were dead. He was so kind to me, Jim, so kind."

"So then you were married."

"Yes."

"But it's different now."

"I can't make you see. I've got to have time, I can't explain—"

"Don't try to arrange things in your mind. Just spit it out."

"But . . . Well, you want me to leave him, don't you?"

"Don't ask such a silly question."

"How can I leave him?"

"How can you *not* leave him? That is, if you still love me."

"But Marcus—"

"What earthly reason would Marcus have for wanting to keep a wife he's not in love with? If he's the decent kind of guy he's supposed to be, all we have to do is tell him."

"No, no! Listen! Sit down! Sit down!"

She sat down herself and waited, and finally he sat down too, across the room. "Now then." She marshaled the unwelcome arguments that came crowding up, defeating her before she more than recognized them. "You've got to give me time—that's one thing. I've done my best to make him happy—and he's tried to make me happy, too, Jim, remember that. But he misses his interest in politics. He gave up everything except his law office. Now I think, I really think, he may consider running for office again. That's where he is tonight. There's a dinner being given by some party leaders and friends from his home state. They may urge him to run for office again, and I think he might decide to do it. I can't ask him to let me go now!"

Jim said, "Why not?"

"*You* know! More talk, more for the opposition to get its teeth into. He's liked and respected, but during a campaign people will say almost anything. Another young wife. Another . . . not scandal, but scandal could be made of it if there was a divorce! There were whispers about Rose's murder, and they would all come to life again. People would say—oh, anything. He's so terribly vulnerable. I can't hurt him like that, Jim, I just can't."

Jim took a long breath, rose, poured himself another drink and went back to his chair. "Well, now then, let's consider it. In some ways you may be right, but in other ways I think you're wrong." He sat there, frowning, looking absently at his glass and turning it around and around in his brown hand.

The miracle of his return gripped her again; her throat ached to cry again from sheer joy. It was all she could do to keep from saying, "I'm ready to go with you anywhere—now, this minute."

Finally Jim said, "If you went to Marcus and told him that I'm alive and want to marry you, and if you still love me—and I think you do—"

She wouldn't say it, but he looked up and knew. "You do still love me," he said quietly. "Marcus Desart being the kind of man you tell me he is, he wouldn't want to hold you. He'd make it easy for you. He wouldn't want to keep you from marrying me, would he?"

"No. No, he wouldn't. But—"

"All right then. I'll talk to him myself."

"I told you, he isn't at home."

Unexpectedly a glimmer of Jim's wry humor twinkled in his face. "Polk told me that. I must say I was glad. I'd been bracing myself to meet him."

Polk had been the front doorman at night for as long as Sue could remember. Every taxi driver, every chauffeur, everybody in the neighborhood, everyone in the city, she sometimes thought, knew Polk.

"Did Polk know you right away?"

"Know me!" Jim laughed. "He turned green. I thought he was going to faint, his eyes popped so. I took him by the shoulders and then, bless his old heart, he hugged me like a father. He said, 'You'll want to see Mrs. Desart.' He said that Mr. Desart had gone out, but that you were in and of course would want to see me. I told him to announce me over the house phone, and then he sent the elevator man off on some errand and brought me up here himself."

Of course Polk had remembered Jim. He'd liked Jim;

he'd got many a taxi for them while they were falling in love.

Jim knew what she was thinking. He said, "I didn't know what love was then, Sue. I thought I was in love, oh, I knew, but now—"

"I know. Jim—"

The tide was too strong. He came to her and took her in his arms. The room ceased to exist; everything vanished into some remote limbo, everything but Jim's presence, his mouth and his arms. He was alive, and nothing else mattered. She whispered, "Yes, yes, I'll go with you."

Jim brought himself back to reality sooner than she. He took her hands and said unsteadily but firmly, "No, Sue. Not this way. We've got to do it the right way. I'm going now, Sue."

He released her hands; he turned away and went across the gallery, his tall figure quick and erect against the wall of green curtains. She would have run after him and tried to stop him, but she knew that he was right. Then it was too late; the door downstairs opened and closed.

chapter 5

Sue sat down. She must think it all out, she told herself, but she could think of nothing except the fact that Jim was alive and that only a moment ago he had held her in his arms. She was in the dazzled state of bewilderment of one who has witnessed a miracle. But though her stored-up love for Jim was almost as dazzling in its sudden release, the barrier remained, all the same.

Jim was a decent and honorable man. She had always thought of herself as being decent and honorable. He had said that there was a right way. They owed it to themselves and to Marcus to find that way. First, Marcus would have to be told of Jim's return. If her husband clung to his decision never again to enter politics, then she could tell him at once about Jim. Marcus would release her. It could be done quietly and with dignity and without permanently hurting him.

But if Marcus was induced to re-enter politics tonight, what then? she thought.

The little French clock on the mantel struck once, and Sue looked up at it. It was an antique, old and wheezy and charming; its walls were glass and its lovely enameled pendulum could be seen, wagging cheerfully back and forth in spite of its age. The brass hearth tools, poker, tongs and tiny shovel, were antique too; the design was French, elaborate and garlanded, and the tongs and shovel handles did not quite match the poker. She counted the chimes of the clock; it was eleven o'clock.

Sue went to the terrace doors and opened them. There were lights in brackets along the terrace; she touched the switch beside the door and the terrace sprang into eerie view. The tiny green leaves shone along the hedge. The awning supports looked bare and skeleton-like. The drooping willows made a faint yellow glow. It seemed years since she had stood in that doorway and seen Marcus on the parapet, leaning over and looking down.

The salmon-pink geraniums were pale in the faint light. She avoided them and the boxes of ivy and walked back and forth. The lights of midtown Manhattan were clear and brilliant. The night air was freshening, and in her green silk dress she was shivering with cold.

She went inside and closed and bolted the terrace doors. She wouldn't talk to Marcus tonight at all; he'd see that she was different. Something stronger than reason, deeper than instinct warned her. She must discover the right approach to Marcus; she must not talk to him until she had gained full control of herself and knew exactly what to say. She must know, too, what had been decided that night.

The French clock had struck several more times before Marcus came home. Woody was with him, and she could hear the voices of the two men in the living room and the clink of ice in their glasses. Their voices were low; they thought she was asleep.

She only realized that Woody had gone when the murmur of voices died away. She didn't hear the private elevator door open or close, but all at once there was only silence. Probably Marcus had tiptoed into his room, hoping not to wake her.

She thought that she could never go to sleep, but she woke once when rain pattered down again upon the terrace. She knew at once that something important and wonderful had happened, and then as the fog of sleep left her she *knew* what it was. In a few minutes, thinking of Jim, she drifted off to sleep again.

Marcus had gone when she awoke, late in the morning. She felt a shamed sense of relief because he had left the house and she could put off meeting his too searching, too intelligent gaze for at least a few hours. Jim was alive; when she thought of that, nothing else seemed to matter. But that was wrong; Marcus had to come first. Sometimes, though, when she looked at it in another way, Jim came first.

It was a gray, half-misty, half-rainy day. At breakfast, Pauline, who had always brought Rose's breakfast tray to her in bed promptly at eight, indicated subtly that she was rising very late. Sue said good morning, and remembering "ze cinema" across an immense abyss of time, asked if Pauline had enjoyed it.

"Oh, no," Pauline replied, dropping her French accent as easily as a glove. "It was lousy. I left it and came home early. Madame had a caller." She gave Sue a bright, penetrating glance. "I heard his voice."

"An old friend," Sue said. "This coffee is cold, Pauline."

Pauline's black eyebrows drew together, but she took the coffee back to the kitchen. The telephone rang; Pauline picked up the extension in the pantry and came out, her black eyes sparkling. "Madame wishes to speak to you."

She meant Belle Minot, Rose's mother. In addressing Sue, Pauline frequently used the third person and said Madame, but in fact there was only one person in Pauline's view who deserved the title—Belle Minot. It had been Belle who advertised for her, investigated her references and employed her for Rose, and the two of them still kept on good terms. Sometimes Sue suspected that Pauline had a neat way of reporting to Belle everything that happened in the Desart household. It would have to be a very neat and delicate way, for Belle would never inquire or even show that she was listening. Yet it would have been almost impossible for her to feel no interest at all in a household where her daughter had been murdered and the killer had never been found, and where her son-in-law had acquired a new, young wife.

Belle liked Sue, and her voice over the telephone was kind, as always. She would be in the neighborhood about noon; might she stop in to see her?

Sue really didn't want to see Belle that day. She didn't want to see anyone who might conceivably guess the secret of what had happened to her. Not that it could remain a secret very long. For a little while, though, until she could talk to Marcus, she wanted Jim's return to remain private. But she felt she had to invite Belle to luncheon.

No, Belle couldn't stay for lunch. She had an engagement. But she'd stop in about noon.

When Sue went upstairs it was still drizzling; the boxes of pink flowers were very bright and looked as if they enjoyed the rain. She had scarcely got upstairs when Woody telephoned; she answered, thinking for a wild moment that it might be Jim. Woody said, "Did Marcus tell you? He gave in. He's going to try for office! He's going to run for senator! I want to see you and tell you all about it."

In her heart she had known it would happen. Woody waited, but she said nothing, and he went on. "It's great news, isn't it? Actually, of course, they've been working for it—all his friends. They've been doing the spadework for months. Of course, he'll have to go home soon to see to things directly. Eventually he'll have to start campaigning actively, but everything will run on greased wheels—that is, unless there's some snag that we don't know about. Are you glad?"

She knew of one snag.

Woody said, again, "May I come over?"

She must have said yes before putting down the telephone. So that was settled. She paced up and down again, thinking. If Marcus ran for office it meant that he must return to his home state quickly. Even if, as Woody said, the spadework had been done without Marcus' knowledge, the time was still short.

She wished that her husband had not decided to run for office, and knew it was a hopeless and selfish wish. But there was Jim to consider, too. She loved Jim. But Marcus needed her. She could not now ask Marcus for a divorce. The only alternative was to ask Jim to wait.

But how long would that be, she thought in despair. If Marcus were elected to the United States Senate, as high and honorable position as there was, it would be all but impossible to ask him for a divorce. His private life would no longer be private.

She couldn't keep Jim's return a secret forever.

For one bad moment she foresaw a dreary vista of years in which she played her role as Marcus' wife and hostess. Jim would grow tired of waiting; she couldn't ask him to wait.

Besides, there would be other women—she's have to expect that. And eventually there would be one woman who would take her place with Jim.

She walked up and down, up and down.

The long, lovely room was gloomy that dark morning, and the scent of the mass of lilacs was almost too sweet and heavy. She turned on the lights. Rose's day book still lay on the table; it seemed to reproach her for failing Marcus.

She didn't hear the doorbell, but Pauline came briskly up the stairs, a slip of paper in one hand. Sue knew exactly what it said; in Pauline's spidery French handwriting there would be scribbled Woody's name. It was Pauline's custom. Whether Sue was alone or there were guests, it made no difference; Pauline brought the name of anyone telephoning or calling, written out on a slip of paper, as if it were the most delicate message which nobody but Sue or Marcus must know. It was so discreet that it suggested the maddest of indiscretions. Sue couldn't break Pauline of the habit; indeed, she hadn't tried very hard to come to grips with any of the maid's customs, for Pauline was faithful and efficient, and she had stayed with Marcus throughout the investigation into Rose's murder and now after his marriage to Sue.

Pauline whisked a small silver tray from behind her apron, deposited the slip of paper upon it and tendered it to Sue, who as a rule had a hard time keeping her face straight during this conspiratorial little routine. She had no inclination to laugh this time, however, for the slip of paper announced Jim's arrival. Pauline had apparently attempted to translate "Commander" and had given it up and scribbled Mr. Loke.

Woody was on his way; Belle was due to arrive; in short, the fat would be in the fire before she was prepared for it.

But she had to see Jim, must reassure herself, look at him, touch him, make sure that he was no dream.

Pauline had seen Rose's day book. She said, "Oh, *la pauvre madame*." Her black eyes glittered; her thin nose grew thinner. "La, la, so bad. Ah, it was le Bon Dieu sent me to the cinema that day. If I had been here . . ." She widened her eyes and Sue expected her to say that she might have saved Rose's life. Instead she said, practically, "He might have killed me too!"

It was a little more than Sue could accept, even from Pauline. She said shortly, "If you had not gone to the movie, Mrs. Desart would not have been alone." Then she realized that she had been unfair; quick, shallow tears came into Pauline's black eyes.

"Madam, how could anyone know!"

"I'm sorry, Pauline. I didn't mean that. Now, tell the Commander—"

"I'll just take the book back to the kitchen."

Pauline reached for Rose's book, but Sue put her hand on it. "No, not yet, Pauline. I need some addresses."

"But, madame, the recipes, I need them—"

"Yes, of course. I'll give it to you soon. But now tell the commander to come upstairs—"

"I'm here," Jim said, strolling across the gallery.

It really was Jim, no doubt about it. Sue's heart sang. It was as if there was nothing between them except that full tide of love. This morning he wore his blue uniform, with the gold stripes on the sleeves and insignia on his shirt collar. The same tide of feeling caught him, for he laughed as if neither of them had a care in the world and took her hands.

"You're in uniform," she said, stumbling, hunting for words until Pauline left.

Jim laughed again, in the same young, carefree way.

"Sure, I had a look at myself in my civvies. That suit I wore yesterday hung like a sack. I blew myself to a couple of new suits this morning. I've lost some weight, naturally. Rice and—rice mainly."

"Thank you, Pauline," Sue said over her shoulder. The green sweep of curtains had been opened early in the morning; the gray light from the sky fell clearly upon Jim's face and she knew every angle of it, every expression, every slightest curve. Pauline's skirt rustled slowly across the gallery and down the stairs. Sue had a notion that her black head was disappearing very slowly, like a Cheshire Cat, but leaving behind her keen ears instead of the cat's grin.

Jim said, suddenly sober, "I had to see you again. Have you talked to Marcus?"

"Oh, Jim, he decided last night. He's going to run for office."

Jim looked at her for a moment, turned, walked to the window and looked out. Finally he said, "What do you want to do?"

"I don't know what to do! This makes a difference. I told you."

"Yes. Yes, it does make a difference, yet—" He turned back to her. "I'll go and see Marcus. We have to think of ourselves but we have to think of him too. I'll go to his office."

She felt a sense of dread. "Jim, can't you wait, just a little, a few days? So we can plan and think it over and—"

"It wouldn't change anything," Jim said quietly.

chapter 6

No, Sue thought, time wouldn't really change anything. Sooner or later she must face Marcus with the fact of Jim's return.

Jim said, "I'll go now. Oh, I forgot to tell you last night. I'm staying at the club if you should want to talk to me." He looked toward the gallery as voices and footsteps came briskly along it. Sue whirled around too, and there were Woody and Belle. Belle's flowery hat was perched on her pretty head; Woody was smiling. They could not have come at a worse moment.

Inwardly she cursed Pauline for having sent them up, this time without her usual overdiscreet announcement, but Pauline had never announced Belle, and she and Woody must have come up together in the elevator. Sue stiffened her back, and to her horror found her throat so dry that she could barely greet them.

Belle was smiling and gurgling at Woody in the charming, flirtatious way that was natural to her, but which her innate good taste prevented from becoming too coquettish. She was utterly unlike Rose, who could never have gurgled or flirted. Woody was smiling too; men always smiled at Belle. Then they both saw Jim, and their faces went puzzled and blank. Sue forced herself to introduce them.

Jim bowed correctly and took Belle's fluttering gloved hand. There was an instant's flicker of something like recognition in Woody's eyes; he had a memory for names. Belle's pansy-brown eyes seemed fixed and thoughtful too, though she smiled bewitchingly and said that she always adored a Navy uniform. Said in Belle's delightful frank way, as if laughing at her own coquetry, it sounded charming and not at all silly.

The look of knowledge in Woody's eyes was now quite clear. He said, "I think I've heard of you, Commander Locke. It seems to me—why, yes! Am I right, Sue? Is this your friend who was shot down in Vietnam? Why, this is wonderful!" He didn't wait for confirmation, but took Jim's hand and shook it. "This is splendid! What happened? A mistake, obviously. I've got to hear the whole story. How long have you been back?"

"Not long," Jim said. "It was lucky for me, yes. Sue, I have an errand downtown—"

But Belle broke in and now the look in her pretty face was knowing. "My dear man, you must tell us everything! Is it true? Did they think you were killed? And then you came back! How perfectly miraculous! See here, my children, I must hear everything!" Whenever Belle wished to be particularly winsome or when she had some ax to grind, she looked very lovely and said "my children." Sometimes Sue suspected that she did it not only to disarm anybody listening to her, but also to emphasize her look of youth rather than of age.

In fact, Belle was about Marcus' age and looked far younger. She was so unlike Rose, it was hard to believe that she had been her daughter. Belle was pretty, delicate, feminine and fragile-looking—but there was nothing fragile about her. Jim looked at her with absent eyes, thanked her—for what Sue didn't quite know—and said that he had to go.

Sue said, "I'll see you down the stairs, Jim."

There was another flicker of interest in Woody's eyes, and Belle's smile was a little fixed. Jim said that there was no need. "I know my way," he said. Sue knew that Belle and Woody had both caught the implication, but Jim, unaware, walked across the gallery and ran down the stairs.

It really couldn't have been worse, Sue thought glumly. Perhaps in a way, though, it was better, for it decided one thing: Marcus would have to be told of Jim's return. But Jim himself was going to tell Marcus, and in her heart she knew that it was the only right course to take.

Belle was in a fluttery mood, waving her white-gloved hands, walking lightly on her high-heeled pumps around the room, touching this and that, looking pretty and smart in her spring suit with its short skirt which showed her slender legs. Woody was flapping at his pockets for a cigarette. He saw the big green bowl of cigarettes on the table, said, "May I help myself?" and strolled over to take a cigarette and light it. Belle threw a glance at Sue over her shoulder. "What a charming young man! But a little abrupt, isn't he?"

Woody came to Sue's rescue. "You'd be abrupt too,

Belle, if you'd had the kind of experience he's had. He was really reported dead, wasn't he, Sue?"

"Yes."

Belle's gentle face could be determined and hard when she was on the scent of something. "Oh, did you know him, Woody? I thought you seemed to meet for the first time."

"I didn't know him. I remembered that Marcus told me something about him. He's—" Woody drew on his cigarette until it glowed redly, and said, looking carefully away from Sue and down at the table, "He's an old friend of Sue's."

Sue nodded. No use trying to explain anything.

Woody said, "He's a very lucky man. Sometime I'd like to hear the whole story. Meantime, we've got great news, Belle. Marcus decided last night. He's going to run for the Senate—that is, of course, if everything goes all right. Naturally, there are some party politics to work out, but I think it's settled."

Belle sat down, folding her hands. "That *is* news. So Marcus has changed his mind? Or"—she smiled—"did you change it for him?"

Woody sat on the arm of Marcus' big chair. "Perhaps he's always regretted his decision to retire."

Belle shrugged daintily. "Did you influence him, Sue?"

"I would have tried to," Sue said flatly. "As it happened, I didn't."

"I'm not so sure of that," Woody said as he rose to get an ashtray. "You insisted upon his going to see those men from his home state last night. Once there, naturally, everybody worked on him. There'll be a few people to . . . well, persuade. There are always a few little internecine battles. But, in fact, almost everything has been done. We've been planning this for a long time."

"We?" Belle said.

Woody shrugged. "People who like Marcus, naturally.

The wheels of politics get under way slowly, Belle, as you know. But once well started it takes only a little momentum for them to roll under full power. The push of Marcus' decision is almost all that we need. Of course, he'll have to go home and campaign. You and Sue will go with him, I hope."

"But Senator—" Belle hesitated and waved one small hand. "Oh, I can never think of his name—the man who was elected instead of Marcus. He's not going to like this."

"Stidger," Woody said.

"Oh, yes. Silly of me not to remember. But then he hasn't done anything to make himself memorable, has he?"

"You've answered yourself, Belle. That's one of the reasons they want Marcus."

"You want him too, obviously," Belle said in her high sweet voice, eying Woody. "It seems to me that if Marcus goes to Washington you might go with him. Is that a possibility?"

Woody returned to the chair, sat down and adjusted a crystal ashtray carefully upon his knee. Sue guessed that he was controlling his words and his temper. "My dear Belle," he said after a moment, "I have a good law practice here."

"Oh, I know. But you did go all the way home to help Marcus during his first campaign, didn't you? You all but commuted between there and New York with Marcus. You must be interested in politics to some extent."

"I was interested, certainly. Marcus is a sound man and he's my friend."

Belle sighed, touched her pretty hat and said lightly, "You know, I would have expected you to go to Washington with Marcus the first time—if he had been elected."

Woody smiled. "I doubt it. I had barely got my feet wet

in politics. He would have needed somebody with more experience. Besides, he had helped me get my practice started and going well. He knew I wouldn't want to leave that."

"Oh, of course. Nobody really wants to be just an errand boy," Belle said, changing her course as easily as a breeze. "Marcus had a wonderful secretary in his office at home. This will please her."

Woody said, "You mean Jean Wilson?"

"Why, yes." There was something just a little too blank about Belle's pretty face. "Why, yes," Belle said. "That was her name. Devoted to Marcus, really. What's happened to her?"

Woody said, "I think she went to Washington to work for Senator Stidger."

"Lucky man," Belle said. "She's a very efficient woman." She returned to Woody. "If Marcus is elected and if he should ask you to go to Washington with him as—well, I don't know as what—" She sighed. "Secretary? Administrative assistant? Special assistant? All such useful titles, aren't they? I never know quite what they mean. But in any event, Woody, if Marcus is elected and asks you to go to Washington with him, will you go?"

Only Belle, Sue thought, could ask such point-blank questions about somebody's private business.

Woody said lightly, "He hasn't asked me, and he hasn't been elected yet. For heaven's sake, Belle, there are still some hurdles—easy ones, I think, but hurdles."

Belle thought for a moment, shrugged and turned to Sue. "Is Marcus happy about this decision of his?"

Sue was thinking of Jim and wondering if he had yet reached Marcus' office. Pulling herself to attention, she replied, "I suppose so. I hope so. I didn't see him this morning. He'd gone when I came downstairs."

"Dear Marcus," said Belle as the doorbell rang loudly, pealing up the spiral stairs.

Belle lifted her delicately arched eyebrows. "Another caller, Sue? You're very popular this morning." Her gentle brown eyes proclaimed her curiosity.

Woody chuckled. "Whoever it is, Pauline is trying to write out his name on that ridiculous little paper pad she carries. She's about to give up on me, but it must rather confuse a stranger. She makes you feel as if this is a jail and she's the wardress—"

"Woody!" Belle said irritably. "Pauline is an excellent servant. I employed her myself."

Sue had scarcely heard the word servant since she was a child. For all Belle's look of slim and lively youth, she was of a different generation and time. Woody's blue eyes met Sue's and guessed her thought and twinkled, as Pauline came up the stairs. She was so excited that she forgot to place the slip of paper on the tray. Her nose was quivering with excitement and she turned on her French accent. "It is ze man. Ze law partner. He say where is Mr. Desart? He say Mr. Desart do not arrive at ze office." She thrust the slip of paper at Sue and stood breathing hard through her thin nose.

Belle cried, "Aubrey Gould! I'm leaving!"

Sue said, "Yes, Pauline, I'm at home."

Woody's eyes were alert. "He wouldn't have come here simply because Marcus hasn't shown up at the office yet."

"No. Of course not," Sue said slowly. "Marcus may have—oh, stopped at his broker's, stopped at the bank, anywhere—"

Woody thrust his wrist out of his Italian silk coat; a gold cuff link shone and his enormous and expensive watch glittered. "It's past twelve." He looked at Sue. "May I—?" He didn't finish, but went swiftly after Pauline.

Belle said, "Woody is attractive, isn't he? I don't understand why some woman hasn't snapped him up by now. But I suppose he's learned to fight them off. You like him, don't you, Sue?"

"Oh, yes, certainly." Sue was trying to listen to Woody as he called down the stairs.

"Hello, Aubrey. Oh—" Woody stopped abruptly. There was a murmur of voices coming up the stairs, and then Woody said, clearly but flatly, "Good morning, Senator."

Belle heard it too. "Senator! Why, that must be . . . Dear me, I can't stand Aubrey Gould, but I wouldn't leave now for anything. Why do you suppose they've come? What's going on?"

Woody reappeared, leading two other men. "Here's Aubrey," he said to Sue. "And this is Senator Stidger. May I present the Senator—Mrs. Desart, Mrs. Minot."

Sue shook hands with both men. Belle fluttered out her hand too, smiling and somehow making her big eyes soft and bright at the same time.

Aubrey Gould pressed Sue's hand warmly and lingeringly, but this was his habit. He saluted Belle with a brief caressing kiss, and her eyebrows went up a little in something like amusement. She had never liked Aubrey. "He's the kind of man who knows the title of every new book and never reads one," she had said once to Sue. "He goes to the opera and has a good sleep, but can talk well afterward about whoever was singing." She added tolerantly, "He's very interested in Aubrey, but he really is a good lawyer."

Aubrey was considerably younger than Marcus and had a dashing manner. He was attractive, though not handsome, tall but rather stocky, blond, with a little too high a color. He was unnaturally spruce and glossy, too carefully tailored to look quite at ease, and had an air of masculine vitality and certainty which somehow suggested that he felt himself a boon to womanhood. Just now, however, he clearly had something on his mind; his pale blue eyes were small and intent.

Senator Stidger was one of those men one could meet a thousand times and still have difficulty in remembering; he was respectable, he was neutral, he would fade into any group. He was very neat, and when Sue motioned them to sit down, he chose a straight chair, adjusted his trimly pressed trousers over bony knees, passed a tidy hand over his gray hair and said nothing.

Aubrey Gould said, "It's sweet of you to see us, Sue. I expected to find you alone."

"Dear me, Aubrey!" Someone must once have told Belle that her laugh was like the tinkle of bells, for occasionally it was so obviously a tinkle that it was off-key. She laughed. "Your tact is as gentle as the kick of a mule. Of course I'll leave, Aubrey. You needn't throw me out." She made no motion to rise, however.

Sue knew that wild horses would have had to drag Belle away, and suppressed a giggle of her own. She was thinking that if Marcus had not arrived at his office, Jim couldn't have seen him. She took a long breath as Aubrey smoothed his shining bright hair and said, "No, no! Really, Belle. Don't leave on my—on our account." His pale eyes shot a glance at the Senator, who looked at nothing.

Woody said, "We'll go, of course. But I really don't think there's any use in your trying to persuade Sue to talk Marcus out of his decision."

"Will you keep your nose out of this, Woody!" Aubrey's face grew pink. "This is for Marcus' good."

"And yours. And, if you'll excuse me, Senator Stidger's."

"What about yourself, my friend!" Aubrey said waspishly. "You got those men to come here and talk to Marcus. You persuaded him to see them. You have some ax to grind—don't try to tell me you haven't."

"And you heard all about it at once. I thought that the Senator was in Washington last night. You must have got hold of him in a hurry in order for him to get the morning plane."

The Senator linked his hands, looked warily at Woody from under dry and wrinkled eyelids and said nothing. Aubrey said tautly, "Suppose I did! Now look here, Woody. I'll put all the cards on the table. Not that you don't know what they are. In the first place, Marcus owes me something. We have a partnership. All the time he was campaigning the first time I carried on in the office for both of us. It wasn't easy. Then when—when he gave that up and came back to work, well, I have to admit *that* wasn't easy either. There were plenty of people to say he had more to do with Rose's murder than anybody ever knew—" He remembered Belle's presence, shot her one look and said, "I beg your pardon, Belle. I wasn't thinking. Rose . . . I mean, this is a sad subject, I realize. I did suggest that you leave."

"You did indeed," Belle said flatly. The prettiness had gone from her face; her eyes were lowered; her youthful figure suddenly seemed all slack and tired. "It's all right, Aubrey. It's—all right. Go on."

Sue went over and sat beside Belle on the sofa, to give her friendly support. But she was thinking only of Jim and of the night before, when for a moment they had forgotten everything but themselves.

The Senator did have a voice after all. He said, "Marcus said he was through with politics. He said he'd never run for office again."

The voice was neutral, the accent vaguely regional; Aubrey's clipped voice rose sharply above it. "That's exactly the point. If Marcus wins the primary, that eliminates Senator Stidger. The Senator accepted this office only with the provision that Marcus had given up all thoughts of any political career."

Belle said sharply, "I doubt if that was a promise!"

Aubrey let out his breath in an angry puff and said to Sue, "I'd like to talk this over with you quietly. But since we have an audience—do you really think it will do Marcus any good to run for the Senate or any other office?"

"Yes," Sue said, and wished bitterly that she could have said no.

"Oh, for God's sake, Sue! Think of the newspapers. Think of the opposition. Think"— Aubrey Gould paused—"of the headlines. The whole dreadful business of Rose's murder will be dredged up again. You can't want that. You can't permit it."

She had encouraged Marcus; she believed that he would be happy only if he re-entered politics. She considered Aubrey's pleas objectively and then shook her head. "No, I don't think that can hurt Marcus."

Belle reached out for Sue and took her hand.

Aubrey looked as if he might burst out of his beautiful custom-made shirt. "You know nothing about it! Nothing—"

There was a faint rumble, which Sue had barely time to recognize before the door of the private elevator opened. Aubrey heard it too and shoved his large body around in his chair; Senator Stidger lifted an inquiring eyebrow; Woody sprang up.

As Marcus came into the room, Sue knew at once that Jim had not talked to him.

chapter 7

Marcus looked exactly as usual; glancing at the roomful of people, he smiled, then came over to Sue and put his hand on her shoulder in a greeting. He nodded to Belle, looked at the three men and said, "I don't need to ask the reason for this meeting. How are you, Senator?"

Senator Stidger looked at Marcus, and the sudden red flame in his eyes was so unexpected in so colorless a man that Sue was shocked into a realization of how much Marcus' decision to run for office affected not only the Senator but many others.

She was innocent of the ways of politics; she knew nothing of all the interplay of personalities, alliances, feuds and friendships, ambitions, disappointments and stubborn hopes. She was suddenly aware of the quicksands upon which a man in government must tread. Had she been right to want this for Marcus? She thought of Aubrey's angry words: "Think of the headlines . . . the whole dreadful business of Rose's murder dredged up again."

Aubrey was talking "—so it's perfectly obvious, Marcus. I came—we came to talk to your wife. I hoped she'd see things more clearly. I'll be frank with you, I'm against this idea of your running for office."

Marcus turned to the Senator. "It was good of you to come to see me," he said in his smooth and courteous way. "I had intended to call on you in Washington before we made any moves."

The tidy Senator was not so unobtrusive after all. Two scarlet streaks appeared on his cheeks. "You promised to stay out of politics, Marcus. You promised—"

Marcus cut in smoothly, yet as ruthlessly as a knife. "I promised nothing." Aubrey and the Senator both started to speak, but Marcus flung up so decisive a hand that it stopped them. Sue saw a rim of grime, like dust, on the edge of Marcus' white cuff; she noted it only because as a rule he was immaculate. His voice rose a little, and its resonance and command filled the room. "I made no promises. It's true that I did not intend to try for elective office again. I've changed my mind. That is all there is to it."

Aubrey shot to his feet, his face scarlet. "Now look here, Marcus, you can't dismiss us like that! You're not being fair to the Senator or to me. I've put up with too much from you as it is—"

"Do you wish to dissolve our partnership?" Marcus cut in. "Nothing could be simpler. We'll set about it today."

Aubrey backed off. "I didn't say—that's a serious step—"

"If you don't mean it, don't suggest it." Marcus' voice was sharp and hard again. "Now then, we've said all that there is to be said—except for one thing, Senator. If after thinking it over, you still think I'm not fair to you, take a look at your record of performance." Suddenly Marcus was smooth and pleasant again. "You force me to say this in the privacy of my own home. I should not like you to force me to say it publicly so that our entire state hears me."

The streaks of red left the Senator's face; ashy white, he shot out of his chair toward Marcus. "You're a liar! I'll make you apologize. You lie—"

Belle squealed. Woody leaped forward between the two men. Aubrey moved too, so quickly that he slipped, off balance, clutching at the table and knocking Rose's day book to the floor. Woody stood quietly in the midst of what was not a scuffle, but what came so close to being one that the room might just have witnessed a brawl.

Swiftly, Woody said, "We'll have lunch, talk it over." Walking between the Senator and Marcus, he had his hand under the Senator's thin and wiry arm; though he didn't herd the three men into the elevator, the effect was the same. The door closed after them.

Sue wondered wildly what would happen if the brawl erupted in the small confines of the elevator. But it wouldn't; they'd had time to reflect.

Belle stared at the door as the hum of the elevator died away. "Whee!" she said. "I thought there was going to be a fight." She sounded frankly disappointed.

"Marcus?" Sue was surprised. "He wouldn't get into a fight like that!"

"You don't know Marcus." Belle opened her smart little bag with a click. "He can be mean."

"Marcus?" Sue said again. "Why, he's always kind and self-controlled and—"

"Oh, darling! You're hero-worshiping. But then of course you've been married such a short time that you haven't seen the other side of him." Belle opened a gold cigarette case, and added, "Somebody ought to tell him to look out for his blood pressure. And look out for yourself, my dear. When the storm blows up—and it does blow up without much excuse sometimes—get out. I've known Marcus a long time, remember. I wonder what he's got on the Senator," she said casually and snapped a tiny lighter.

"Belle!" Sue cried again in remonstrance and surprise. But at the same time she knew that Belle, nobody's fool, had seen something of politics and a great deal of Marcus. She hoped that Jim would not encounter Marcus in this mood. Anything could happen.

But the four men were going to lunch together. Woody would keep the lid on.

Besides, Jim must have arrived at Marcus' office by now, and somebody would have told him that Marcus was not there. By now Jim would have long since gone. Of course, he might have left his name. That would be enough for Marcus. But she must keep them apart until—until, she thought, she herself had decided something.

Belle's lighter wouldn't work. "Out of fluid," she said. "It's always out of fluid. I forget to fill it. But I hate to carry a big lighter in my bag." She rose as lithely as a girl; one small foot advanced before the other in her graceful move. Picking up the handsome Royal Doulton table lighter on the table, she looked at it thoughtfully. "I gave that to Marcus once for his birthday." As she lit her cigarette, she saw Rose's day book on the floor. "Oh." She stooped to pick it up. "Rose's—" She put it back on the table, then flipped over some pages. The youth had gone from her face again; her trim figure slumped a little. "She kept everything here, you know. Recipes—" A puzzled note came into her voice. "Where was this?"

"I think in the kitchen or pantry, somewhere. Marcus got it out so I could look up some addresses. The florist, you know, for the terrace boxes, and the awning storage place."

"Oh, yes." Belle turned to look out at the terrace. "You've got the same arrangement," she commented, as Woody had said. "Salmon-colored geraniums and ivy. It's very pretty," she added without a quaver.

Sue said suddenly, "I admired her very much. But she wasn't a bit like you."

Belle's slender shoulders gave a little shrug, and she moved to look at herself in the distant mirror at the end of the gallery. It gave Sue a pang when she saw Belle lift her head and straighten her back in an effort to shed the years and, perhaps, the memory of tragedy. She turned then to Sue, her soft brown eyes thoughtful. "No, Rose and I were not at all alike. She was like her father—a good thing, really. Her father was very handsome, very rich, fun to be with, like his Spanish mother. He looked rather like her, too. Very self-possessed and stately. Yes, Rose was like him. Yet, you know, in some ways I think that I am more prudent than Rose was. I have a stronger sense of self-preservation."

This was a new and surprising comment on Rose's character. Sue wanted to question the older woman, but she felt restrained. Belle had always spoken of Rose in a matter-of-fact way, which certainly was preferable to ostentatiously avoiding her name. But she had never before spoken of her daughter in this way.

Belle said, still thoughtfully, "No, I'm not at all reckless or daring. Not that Rose was that. Still, under all that air of calm and cool poise—yes, she was impulsive. Our only child, and perhaps she was a little too much indulged." She looked at Sue directly. "We've never talked about the murder," she said flatly. "People never ask me what I think—that is, not now. Of course, during the investigation the police and detectives asked me everything they could think of. My friends in New York didn't ask me in so many words, but they might as well have done so. People wrote to me from home but they were very tactful. You've never said a word about it."

"Belle! I wouldn't have—"

"Oh, I know. You like me. You wouldn't have hurt me as that ass Aubrey Gould did."

"I liked Rose. I didn't know her well, but well enough to like her. Well enough to try very hard to . . . not to take her place, but to do my best to make Marcus happy."

"I've seen that. I don't mind saying now that when Marcus wrote me a note and said you were going to be married—he'd have done better to come and talk to me, but I expect it was easier for him to write it—in any event, I'll not say that I was pleased. Not right away. But then as I thought it over, I realized that it was, first, nothing I could control and, second, nothing that I wished to control. Marcus' life is his own. I've made my own life here too, and I don't depend on Marcus' friendship. So I wrote a note of congratulations, and then he invited me to meet you. Now—well, if you want to know, I've been very pleased about the whole thing."

It was like Belle to finish on an unsentimental, almost brusque, note.

"Thank you. Thank you for all your goodness to me too." For an instant Sue was caught by a fantastic desire to tell Belle about Jim's intention of talking to Marcus. On the surface Belle was coquettish, feminine, airy as a feather; underneath she was smart as tacks and, Sue suspected, as hard as nails. Certainly she was both wise and worldly wise, and behind her mask of prettiness and coquettishness she was coldly realistic. But of course it wouldn't be right to tell Belle what Jim's return meant until Jim had talked to Marcus. She felt chilled again when she thought of their meeting and of the astonishing capacity for anger Marcus had displayed only that morning.

Belle said, "Oh, we understand each other, you and I. I'm going to tell you something I've never breathed to a soul. I was wrong—I wasn't in a state to be very reasonable—but at first, after my daughter was murdered, it did occur to me that she and Marcus might have had one of their tempestuous quarrels, that it had got out of hand and—well, more violent and—there, my dear, sit down again. I told you I was wrong. Don't look so scared. I shouldn't have said that even to you."

Sue sat back down on the sofa; she hadn't realized that she had jumped up until she felt the light pressure of Belle's hand. But she had to ask, "Did they quarrel often?"

Belle was airy. "Oh, I don't think so. It's not important—"

"What did they quarrel about?"

"Why, I . . . Well, you see Rose was so much younger than Marcus. Naturally, Rose liked—oh, entertaining, that sort of thing. And all at once she was living in a great, cosmopolitan city where there were so many interests. And Marcus—why, Marcus is older than I am—" Belle paused and said, "Not that I consider myself on the shelf, and I don't intend to! Now forget what I said. I was wrong to think it and wrong to tell you. The truth must be that Rose in her self-confident way simply answered a doorbell without asking who it was first. The usual sordid story—a prowler, attempted robbery, anything. He probably came prepared for violence, and then when he realized he had killed her, he ran away."

Sue swallowed hard. "Nothing was taken."

"No, except perhaps for some cash in Rose's handbag. Nobody was sure. She had withdrawn it the day before; they had the check and the teller at the bank remembered her."

"I'd forgotten that. It was—"

"Five hundred dollars. Enough to make robbery worthwhile, I suppose. Not murder. But as I told you, Rose was too sure of herself, too self-confident. She'd have fought for the money or a jewel or anything, simply because she wouldn't give it up." There was a pause, and then Belle said, "I suppose sometime we had to have this talk. Although—" In a flash she was herself again, her eyebrows drawn in a puzzled half-frown. "I'm sure I don't see exactly why we'd have had to talk of it. People are always saying that something unpleasant must be talked about, when really it shouldn't be—not ever! Do you like my hat? First time I've worn it. Seems to take several times to discover how to wear a new hat. And—" She put out her cigarette, signaling her departure.

Sue rose and walked with her along the gallery. "And how to get along with a husband," Belle added merrily. "Mind me now. If you see signs of a storm from Marcus, run for cover. Actually, if I were you, the minute Marcus gets a certain look, I'd go out and take a nice long walk. He'll have calmed down by the time you return."

They were going down the stairs, Belle first, betraying her real age again, touchingly, by clinging to the railing. She sighed. "Well, now you and I will have to go back home and rally around Marcus. You'll like the people, and that will make it all easier for you."

Nothing was going to be easy, Sue thought. At the door she asked a question which had been hovering in the air. "Belle, you said you wondered what Marcus had on the Senator. It sounded almost like—well, like a form of blackmail. Marcus wouldn't—"

Belle patted her cheek. "You are a baby. Good-bye, dear. I'll call you about the concert next week. We have a date for luncheon."

As she went out into the foyer, the elevator door was just closing, and she cried out, "Wait, wait for me," like a girl. The operator smiled, and Belle stepped gaily into the elevator, waving at Sue as if she hadn't a care in the world. Her pretty face and smart new hat and white-gloved hands vanished as the door closed.

Sue went quickly up the stairs. She had many things to think about and her whole life's course to decide, but first she must try to find Jim. He must be stopped from seeing Marcus today. Her husband was in no state of mind to hear of Jim's return and to consider reasonably its effect upon Sue and on himself.

Perhaps she could reach Jim by telephone. Though Pauline's ears could be abnormally sharp and though there was a kitchen extension, Sue decided that she must take the risk. She remembered the telephone number for Jim's club; she could never forget it; her finger dialed the number almost automatically. But Jim was not there.

chapter 8

As the day went on, Sue took some comfort from the fact that nobody telephoned, for she had a notion that if Jim and Marcus met, she would hear of it at once. At intervals she tried Jim's club again. She had lunch downstairs from a tray. Pauline said something about going out, eying Sue tentatively, and she nodded permission. She went to the terrace and resolutely transplanted a few more flowers. The clouds were hanging low overhead, and the flowers seemed absurdly bright and gay. It was an odd kind of day; the whole city seemed to take on a kind of anonymity, a gray dullness into which Marcus and Jim had vanished. It began to drizzle.

At last, a little after three, the private elevator hummed. She ran into the living room in time to see the door open and Jim walk out. Marcus was behind him. He ushered Jim into the room, motioned politely to a chair, said something about cigarettes or a drink, and saw Sue.

"Ah, Sue, my dear. There you are." He gestured toward Jim, who stood like a rock, looking at Sue. Marcus said in his warm orator's voice, "This young man—Commander, isn't it?—yes, my wife, Mrs. Desart. Now then, suppose we sit down and you can tell me what's on your mind. I'm always glad to be of any assistance to our young men in the service. Not that I can do much at the moment, you know. Still, I have some friends who may be able to oblige you."

Jim, white-faced, stood straight and looked at Marcus. "I'm afraid you didn't hear my name, Mr. Desart. It's Locke. Jim Locke."

Marcus had sat down in his big green chair. Sue was frozen. Her husband's hands suddenly gripped the arms of the chair and he sat forward. "Did you say Locke?"

"Yes, sir. Jim Locke. It was a mistake," Jim said clearly. "I wasn't killed at all. It was a mistake."

There was a long pause. The rumble of traffic from Madison Avenue was suddenly loud. At last Marcus leaned back. "I see. Well, I must congratulate you. A mistake, was it? Sometime you must tell me the whole story. Now do sit down, Commander Locke. I can see that you have something you wish to say."

"Only one thing," Jim said. "I was engaged to Sue. I'm back home. I want—" He took a long breath. "I'll put it briefly, Mr. Desart. Sue and I were engaged—"

"You said that," Marcus interrupted. "But go on. I suppose you want to marry her."

"Yes, I do."

Marcus did not look at Sue, but he said, "You are not surprised, Sue. Clearly you two have met recently. When?"

Sue knew exactly how hard it was for Jim to speak; and

for a moment she thought she wouldn't be able to answer. "Last night."

Marcus' hands gripped the chair arms harder. He still didn't look at her. "Where?"

"Here."

"I see. When I was away."

"Wait a minute, Mr. Desart," Jim said. "She didn't know that I was alive. I came to see her."

"You knew that she had married?"

"Yes. But I had to see her."

Still addressing neither of them, looking into space, Marcus said, "Knowing that she had married, you still had to see her."

"Look here, Mr. Desart," Jim said miserably. "I'm sorry about all this. That is, I really can't apologize for being alive but—"

Marcus broke in. "Why, my dear young man! You should be very glad. I expect you are a hero. Yes, I admire your courage, indeed I do. I am delighted to know that after all you were not killed. This is a very happy thing, very fortunate. It has nothing to do with me, however, and nothing to do with my wife."

"I want you to let Sue marry me."

Marcus laughed smoothly. "That's impossible. She's my wife." He rose, pulling himself up slowly. "I can quite understand your haste to see my wife. I may think it was ill-advised, impulsive, even rash, but I can understand it. Now then, much as I dislike saying this to one of our heroes—" Marcus straightened up and suddenly thundered, "Get out of my house!"

"There's divorce," Jim said, very quietly.

"So you've talked it over. Well, I'll tell you this. Sue cannot divorce me; she has no grounds for divorce. She can leave me if she wants to. She can go and live with you for as long as you can both abide such an arrangement. It cannot be a very happy one. However, she'll never have a divorce. It is a preposterous suggestion. I'm a lawyer. I know some things about law. If you do me the honor—a little belatedly, I must say—to talk to me of divorce, your time is wasted. There will never be a divorce. Now you are in my house. This is my wife. Get out," Marcus shouted again, suddenly. His face was red. "If you don't get out I'll throw you out myself!"

Jim's self-control wavered a little then; Sue caught the flash of anger in his eyes. "I don't think you can," he said very quietly. "I may look a little worn down but I'm in quite good shape really."

"I can call the police! Get out, both of you! Go with him if you want, Sue. Come crawling back to me when you've had enough of the kind of life you'd have to live." Marcus' lips came back from his teeth in a grin that was like a snarl. "That's what you'll do, you know, and I won't have you. But go with him now, if you want to!"

She almost said, "Yes, I'll go this minute." Marcus' ugly smile was as shocking as the glimpse of the other Marcus, a man she had never known, had been only that morning. She actually put out her hand toward Jim, scarcely knowing that she had done so until he, self-controlled again, said, "No, Mr. Desart. We can't do that. Believe me, neither of us wants to hurt you. We really love each other, you know. We are talking about the lives of three people. I'd like to see you again, after you've had time to think things over. I realize that this has been a surprise."

Marcus laughed raucously. "Surprise is not quite the word. However, yes, of course." His manner changed so swiftly and easily that Sue could not quite believe the transformation. He said smoothly, with kindness and warmth in his voice, "I'm sorry, Sue. All this has been a shock, but I'm not cruel. I understand. I've always understood. We'll take time to consider all this." Now he produced the kind smile which Sue knew. "It will affect my decision to run for office again, you see. Not that I would ask you to consider that. But things must be done carefully. That is, prudently and slowly. Sue agrees with me, I think. We need time, all three of us. This has all been very unexpected." To Sue's utter astonishment, he took Jim's arm and led him to the elevator door. "You'll forgive me now. We must . . . there are arrangements, things to work out. Believe me, I am delighted to know that the news of your tragic death was not true."

He had reached into the elevator and pressed the down button. In a moment the door closed, shutting off Sue's view of Jim. As the elevator rumbled downward, Marcus came across the room, looked at her calmly—and slapped her.

The force of the blow knocked her against the sofa, and she slid down into it. As she tried to pull herself up, he slapped her again, on the other side of the face, so hard that her senses seemed to black out. She stared at him, trying to catch her breath; her hands went to her face. He said, "Now that's the end of that. You're not to see this man again. Understand me?"

"You—" she whispered the first thought that shot into her mind—"you killed Rose."

Marcus handsome face turned a queer gray, and he stared at her as if she were a ghost. He said stiffly, moving his lips very slowly, "I'd kill any woman who was unfaithful to me, remember that. Now get in there"—he motioned toward her bedroom—"and wash your face. Put something on it. But don't forget what I said." He walked away from her with heavy footsteps, across the room and down the stairs.

She rose, dizzy, half-unbelieving, and went through her bedroom and into the dressing room. In the mirror she looked at her face. There was a scarlet streak along one jaw. The other slap had been higher, close to her eye; there would probably be bruises. She thought, strangely, that she could show those bruises to a lawyer—Aubrey?—and tell him what had happened. Wasn't physical cruelty a reason for divorce?

Somewhere inside her, common sense began to operate slowly. Time, she thought at last, time. She washed her face with cold water and patted some powder over the red marks. Belle had said, Get out. When you see signs of a storm from Marcus, run for cover.

In any event she could not stay here just now; she had to conquer her anger. Marcus was still downstairs. She took a coat and her handbag, crossed the living room and ran for the small elevator. Marcus did not hear her. When the elevator came, she got into it and pressed the button. She had no idea where she was going.

The lobby was empty; the doorman was busy whistling for a taxi. She went out, crossed Madison and Fifth avenues and walked along the park.

Briefly, she thought of going to Belle, but she couldn't bring herself to do that. She thought of telephoning Jim, but he would guess from her voice that something ugly had happened. Common sense, again, warned her against it. She must have time, must give Marcus time, give Jim time. Nothing could be settled at once. But Marcus was a violent man. Marcus can be mean, Belle had said.

She thought of going to a hotel; the same common sense checked her. She thought of going to Aubrey or to Woody, and knew that this too was unwise. Her first and hardest task was simply to get control of herself. She had felt utter disbelief; Marcus could not have struck her; he could not be two men, each as different from the other as night and day. But her face was tender when she touched it.

She walked aimlessly, up and down the sidewalk bordering the Park. When she became aware of her surroundings, it was almost dusk; lights seemed to spring up suddenly everywhere. All at once she was very tired. There was nothing to do but return home. She had formulated no course of action; she had thought out nothing at all to say to Marcus; she only knew that she wasn't going to run. Whatever happened she must behave with as much dignity as she could summon.

In cold fact, Marcus had justice on his side. He was the husband; he had been kind to her; all the arguments of law and loyalty seemed to array themselves behind him. He had been taken by surprise. He was terribly vulnerable, not only because he had decided only the night before to resume his career, but because his first wife had been brutally murdered. No, justice was on his side. She could not evade that fact.

But Marcus was never going to strike her again. She would never allow it to happen again. Oddly, now she had no fear of him; somehow the other Marcus, the one she knew, had begun to resume his identity. By now this Marcus would be ashamed of his own violence.

Turning into the lobby, she went past the main elevator, groped in her handbag and got out the key to the private elevator. It was at the lobby floor; she was so engrossed, thinking of the coming interview with Marcus, telling herself that whatever happened she must keep her head and her temper, that she was almost unaware of the elevator rising slowly, until it gave a little jar and stopped. She saw nothing in the elevator itself. She came out into the living room and had started across to her bedroom, intending to remove her coat and brush her hair, when she happened to glance out to the terrace. Someone had finished planting all the geraniums and ivy. This surprised her so much that she went across the gallery and out the terrace door. The long porch boxes bloomed with geraniums and ivy. The now-empty florist's flats had been neatly stacked in the corner of the terrace by the gate. There never was a real shadow but the stacks of empty little boxes covered the corner where Rose had died. There was much more light here than down in the dusk of the streets.

The mere fact that all the little pots of flowers and ivy had been emptied and the plants themselves neatly arranged in the terrace boxes was oddly appropriate to the nightmarish afternoon. Pauline would not have finished Sue's chore of planting; she had made it clear that anything to do with the terrace was not her province. So, Sue thought, Marcus must have planted the flowers in an attempt to make peace with her.

She had an odd impression that someone had been on the terrace quite recently; it was almost as if she felt the breath of a presence. Yet there were only the flowers and ivy, the bare awning supports, the boxes of hedge which lined the broad parapet, the rapidly settling dusk of evening.

Then she saw a ball of bright green on the red tiles of the floor. It was the twine used for tying up trees and plants, and instantly she saw that the drooping willow had been tied to one of the awning supports. Its slender branches made a faint yellow haze against the darkening sky. The hedge beside it had been broken a little; a few twigs lay on the tiles beside the green ball of twine. It looked as if someone had fallen through the hedge.

As she started forward the doorbell stabbed the air; it rang and rang and then stopped. The door downstairs must have been flung open, for feet were running up the stairs.

It was a nightmare, and a nightmare's pictures flickered

around her. A policeman in blue uniform ran past her to the parapet and leaned across the broken hedge. Another blue-uniformed figure joined him. Old Duffy, the superintendent for the apartment house, came puffing out too. His face was gray; he had a key clutched in his hand. He ran to the parapet and then faltered, held to an awning support and cried hoarsely, "The terrace! The same place! His wife was murdered right over there!" He waved at the corner of the terrace.

One of the policemen whirled around, saw Sue and came running over to her. He took her arm, led her inside the house, across the gallery, guided her to a chair and put her in it.

He said, "I'm sorry, I'm sorry—"

She thought she spoke; her lips must have made some motion. The young policeman said, "I'm so sorry. The super says it's Mr. Desart. He was found only a few moments ago."

Something shrieked like a lost soul; the wail rose from the murky drizzly street far below. But it was not a lost soul, not Marcus, not anybody. The young policeman said gently, "It's the police ambulance. But I'm afraid it's too late, Mrs. Desart. You see, he must have slipped. He fell. There was nothing anybody could do for him."

chapter 9

Marcus had fallen from the parapet. He had climbed up on it to tie the willow branches. He had slipped and fallen. Everybody said so.

Old Duffy said so, twisting his passkey to the penthouse in his shriveled hand, staring at the now dark sky outside the windows. The policeman said so. A doctor, summoned hurriedly from his office off the lobby floor, said so. When Pauline returned (running up the stairs, for elevator men and porters and doormen had told her what had happened), she said so too. He had fallen.

Pauline telephoned for Belle, who said that she would come immediately.

The young doctor was obviously relieved to know that a member of the family was on her way. Another young man in a gray suit, who seemed to be in a position of police authority, appeared, but the doctor persuaded him to wait until Mrs. Desart was sufficiently recovered from shock before asking her to identify the body.

Old Duffy lifted his gray face from his wrinkled hands. "I identified him. Right away. It's Mr. Desart." He moaned again. "The same penthouse. The same terrace. His wife was murdered there."

The young man in the gray business suit eyed Sue thoughtfully and then introduced himself. "Lieutenant Conti of the police," he said. "Your own identification of Mr. Desart's body can wait, Mrs. Desart. I have to make a report of the accident. Would you mind answering a few questions now, or would you rather wait until morning?"

Sue must have said now. She didn't really know what she said or did; it was all a nightmare. But it was not a dream; it was a fact that Marcus had climbed up on the parapet again, a fact that he had looked down, as he had done the previous day, a fact that he had gone forever in a moment.

Lieutenant Conti sat down beside her. The two capsules the doctor had given her were beginning to make her feel mercifully hazy. The doctor disappeared, escorted away by Pauline, who then returned, like a slim raven in her chic black dress and with her avid black eyes. The uniformed policeman had gone too. Sue was vaguely aware that Lieutenant Conti had spent some time on the terrace with a flashlight, whose beams flashed here and there over the scene.

In the midst of the confusion, old Duffy had gone too. "This to happen in my apartment house, this to happen again," he had groaned, trudging heavily along the gallery.

"I don't know anything about it," she said now to Lieutenant Conti. "I was away. I came home and went out on the terrace and saw the ball of green twine, and then they came. I saw the green twine and then—" She had a dim feeling that she was repeating herself. The young lieutenant said, "Take your time, Mrs. Desart. How do you think it happened?"

"Oh, he fell from the wall, the parapet. He had the green twine."

"You mean the green stuff like yarn he seems to have used to tie up the tree out there?"

"Yes. And yesterday he did it too. That is, he started to tie up the tree and he had climbed up on the wall and then he—he looked down and was dizzy and he promised me he wouldn't try it again."

Pauline said, "Lieutenant, it is all the way Madame says. Mr. Desart climbed up there yesterday and he was giddy and a friend of his, Mr. Woodard, saw it and he got him down and—" Her dark eyes flickered toward Sue. "I happened to be in this room, at the door of the elevator, Madame. It may be that you did not see me. But I heard and saw. I was horrified. I had an attack. I was obliged to go back downstairs and take some brandy. I had a *crise de nerfs* zat very moment," she added, turning on her French accent.

"I see," the young lieutenant said thoughtfully. It seemed to Sue in her now-befuddled state of mind that he did see something or other, for his green eyes were very bright. Certainly he saw that Sue was now in no condition to answer any questions. He said, "I expect the sedative the doctor gave you is taking effect, Mrs. Desart. Please try to relax. This relative, this lady you expect—" He glanced at Pauline, who said quickly, "Yes, yes, Madame Minot. Mrs. Desart's mother-in-law. No, no, that is not right! Mrs. Minot, you see, is the mother-in-law of Mr. Desart."

Lieutenant Conti waited a moment. "You mean, Mrs. Minot is the mother of Mr. Desart's first wife."

Pauline said eagerly, "*Ma pauvre Madame!* She was murdered. Dreadfully. Murdered out there on the terrace."

"Yes," Lieutenant Conti said. "Nearly six years ago."

"Six years in August," Pauline said. "Six years August twelfth. I had gone to ze cinema—"

The lieutenant cut her off neatly. "Yes, thank you. Mrs. Desart, I advise you to try to rest. If I can do anything—"

Pauline interposed again, "I am here, sir. Madame Minot will be here."

The lieutenant rose and shook down his neat gray trouser legs as adroitly as a bird shakes its feathers into place.

Pauline's bright eyes glittered and her thin nose quivered with excitement as she escorted Lieutenant Conti to the stairs. He had barely gone when the doorbell began to ring again, furiously. Pauline hurried down the stairs; there were more voices, and then Aubrey Gould came pounding across the gallery, followed by Woody.

"Belle told me," Woody said. "Sue, I'm so sorry."

"Belle phoned me too," Aubrey said. "This is horrible!" His face looked damp, and his hand was wet when he shook hands with Sue as if he had to do something.

Woody went to look out the window at the terrace as Belle appeared with Pauline. Belle was white and still; she sat down by Sue and said nothing.

Aubrey mopped his face with a handkerchief. "Dreadful. Poor Marcus. A terrible accident."

"The hedge is broken," Woody said. "He must have tied up the willow tree, Sue. He promised you he wouldn't try it again."

Woody's face seemed to fade into the distance and then return again. Sue looked at Aubrey, whose pale blue eyes had sharp black pupils. He had forgotten all about his appearance; he looked only like a middle-aged, well-stuffed tailor's dummy, and he too seemed to fade away and then float back again. It must be the pills, she thought confusedly. She put her hand out and Belle took it. Aubrey was not really in a state of catalepsy, for he moistened his lips and said, "He didn't come back to the office at all. After lunch, you know, Woody and I went back to our offices and Marcus just went off somewhere. He didn't say where, but he wasn't in the office. When did he come home, Sue?"

She heard him clearly and replied, but her words sounded vague. "About three, I think. A little after. And then, later—I went for a walk. A long walk. I had just got back when the superintendent came. And the police."

Belle said, "Hush, dear. Don't talk."

Belle's face was a white mask, but her eyes were alive. Sue couldn't stop. "I had just got home. I went out on the terrace. Marcus had planted the flowers."

There was a puzzled pause. Then Woody said, "Oh, I know." He turned to Aubrey. "There were some little flowers. Lots of them. Sue was going to put them in the boxes along the terrace."

"Marcus planted them," Sue began again, and her voice, like their faces, seemed to waver and fade.

Belle said, "I'll stay with Sue tonight. Come, my dear. No more talk."

Woody said something about identifying the body. "I met a police lieutenant downstairs in the lobby. I told him I'd do it. You needn't think about it, Sue."

Aubrey gave a kind of moan and said that he would go with Woody. "I knew Marcus, and we had a business friendship long before he came to live in New York," he said. "Oh, we had our disagreements. Naturally. But he was my best friend all the same."

Then they were gone and Belle was in her room with her and had closed the door. Belle turned down Sue's bed and got out nightgown and slippers. She shaded the light and then disappeared into the shadows. Sue drifted off. Occasionally something came through the mist; she was aware that Pauline brought in a tray to Belle and told her in a piercing whisper that she must eat. A long time later, Woody tapped lightly at the door, tiptoed in and whispered something to Belle, who put her hand to her face in surprise. "*Who*?"

The mists cleared away a little. Woody said in a low voice, "The young commander, Sue's friend. He phoned. Pauline told him what happened, and he wants to talk to Sue."

Sue struggled up on her elbow and reached for the telephone by the bed, but as she groped for it Woody tiptoed away and suddenly she was back on the pillows again. But she thought, Jim! Jim is alive and home.

Sometime in the night she came sharply to her senses, sat up and looked around her and thought, It was not an accident. Marcus would not have climbed up on the wall again. He knew the danger, and he had promised not to do it. Marcus was prudent. After the near-accident of the previous day he would no more have climbed up on the wall than he would have crossed a busy street against a traffic light in front of a stream of onrushing traffic.

So they were all wrong. It was not an accident. If that was true, there were only two alternatives: suicide or murder.

Murder was no stranger to the terrace. Again she could almost see a shadow at the corner of the terrace.

Nobody would murder Marcus. But he was far too rational a man to commit suicide. Besides, there was no reason, especially with his new political career. But . . .

She had forgotten Belle, who suddenly sat up on the chaise longue, her face peering unexpectedly from the dusk in the corner of the room. A blue eiderdown covered her legs. "Can I get anything for you?"

The words came from Sue's lips as if from a long and subterranean thought process: "It was suicide."

Belle, who was wrapped in Sue's pink dressing gown, hugged it around her as if she felt a chill in the air. "Marcus!"

Again Sue felt that long process of thought. She said, "Marcus loved Rose. He never got over that. Today . . . today he must have been thinking of her because he had decided to run for the Senate. He had to think of her, Belle. All the circumstances of his first campaign and the way it ended in Rose's tragic death—everything. And there was the parapet; he had tied up the tree, he had planted the geraniums and ivy, and all that must have reminded him of Rose. And—and that was it. It *must* have been it. He simply didn't want to go on any more without her."

Belle looked at her seriously. "I don't think you should talk, dear. Go back to sleep." But there was something like a question in her eyes.

Sue said, "What is it? What do you want to say?"

"I'm not sure that I should, or that it's a friendly thing to say."

"Go on."

"Well then, why did you marry Marcus?"

Sue met Belle's eyes steadily, but all her senses warned her of danger. It was clear that Marcus had not confided her own secret to Belle. Sue couldn't now say, I married Marcus because they said that Jim had been killed. I needed Marcus' friendship, I admired him and I knew that I could never love anyone again the way I loved Jim. Marcus and I knew each other's hearts; the marriage was companionship—and it was successful in its way, until this afternoon. She couldn't say that, for Jim had come back.

The ugly scene between the two of them flashed across her memory in every detail.

And then she thought again, If it wasn't an accident, it must be suicide or murder. Nobody would have murdered Marcus, but the police might say that Jim had a motive.

She had to talk to Jim. He must be able to prove that he had not been near the penthouse at the time of Marcus' death.

Belle said, "Forgive me for saying this, Sue. I ought not to speculate about your life. But to be frank, it did occur to me that perhaps something had gone wrong, someone you loved. . . Perhaps you were disappointed, something like that. So you married Marcus on the rebound. And do you know, Sue, when I saw that young naval officer here this morning—no, it's yesterday morning by now—" She broke off and looked at the watch on her small wrist. "Yesterday morning, it seems years ago. But when I saw him, there was something in the air between you. I knew it; really, dear, I knew it. I thought then, That's the man Sue really loves. Then Woody said something about his having been reported dead and I knew that it had been a mistake and that he had returned, and I couldn't help thinking that perhaps this was why you married Marcus. I mean, thinking this young man was killed and feeling heartbroken and all that—one can't help thinking such things. I've said too much, but I've got to say more. Why did Marcus strike you?"

Sue put her hands hurriedly to her cheeks.

Belle's eyes were as cold as ice. "I thought so. Then Marcus knew that this young man had returned. When did they meet? Did he come here? What did you say to Marcus? No!" Belle flung up her hand suddenly, as if to stop any reply. "No, don't answer. It's better not to let anyone know."

She turned abruptly, and went across to the windows, pulled aside the curtains and stood looking out over the dark terrace with its two secrets. Beyond, the lights still glimmered through the blackness of a sleeping city. Presently she said over her shoulder, "It was an accident. We'll never mention suicide or—" She came back to the bed and said very firmly, "Or the young man who came back from the dead. He phoned you last night. We wouldn't let you talk to him."

"I know, I heard."

Belle said, "Now go back to sleep. You've had enough sedation to put you to sleep for a month. Get the good out of it." She had reverted to her usual crisp yet friendly manner. Settling herself on the chaise longue again, she shoved the cushions to a comfortable position, pulled up the eiderdown and shut her eyes.

Belle had shrewdly guessed the truth. But she was Sue's friend. Those marks and bruises on her face must be concealed . . . She sank into a confused gray fog again.

The next morning Lieutenant Conti came again. Though he apologized for taking Sue's time, apologized for everything, he asked questions.

He was still asking his quiet little questions when the phone rang. In a moment Pauline came rustling up the stairs, the discreet little slip of paper in her hand. On it was written in Pauline's crabbed hand, "Mr. Lok."

chapter 10

Sue had to talk to Jim. She would simply have to risk her conversation being overheard by Lieutenant Conti. She said to Pauline, "Thank you. I'll take it in my room. Will you excuse me for a moment, Lieutenant?"

He nodded, and when she went into her bedroom she purposely left the door open, as if to suggest that there was no conversation which she might wish to keep a secret.

After picking up the telephone and waiting in vain to hear the click of the kitchen extension, she said, "Yes, Jim."

"Sue! I phoned last night."

"I know."

"They wouldn't let me talk to you. They told me what had happened. I read about it in the papers this morning. They said it was an accident."

"Yes. He must have climbed up on the wall of the terrace—"

Jim cut in, "Where were you when it happened?"

"I was out for a walk."

Jim was about to question her further; she could feel it over the wire like a tremor. She said, "One of the police—I mean a lieutenant—is here now talking to me about the accident. I do thank you for phoning."

Jim said, "Wait a minute, Sue, everything *is* all right, isn't it? You can answer yes or no."

"I don't know. Thank you so much," she said quickly and put down the receiver.

She didn't dare hope for a moment that the effect of friendly formality she had tried to suggest had deceived Lieutenant Conti. As for Pauline, of course she couldn't be sure that the woman had raced downstairs and applied her ear to the telephone there but she had every reason to feel that Pauline would have felt it quite unnatural to leave any promising path of drama unexplored.

The lieutenant, however, was not in the living room, so she needn't have been so concerned about his listening ears. He was standing out on the terrace, his rather slender figure in a neat and conservative gray suit blocked against the sky. The day was trying to be sunny, but was having a bad time of it, for a cloudy overcast lingered and only occasionally permitted a ray or two of sunlight.

She went to the door of the terrace. The pink flowers and green ivy had taken on the curious, eerie brightness of color which precedes a storm. The lieutenant saw her and walked toward her. She realized that he was older than she had at first thought, or perhaps it was experience which had placed lines around his green eyes and mouth and had put gray in his red hair. He carried himself well; yet there was what seemed to be a tired sag to his broad shoulders. He said, "I'm really very sorry to oblige you to talk to me now, Mrs. Desart. It's a formality, merely for my report. But we'll postpone the inquest for a time."

"Inquest! Oh, I see—because it was an accident."

"Yes, of course. It's the law," he said patiently. "Duffy will have to testify about finding him. We may be able to find a witness, though we haven't yet. You arrived home about when?"

"I don't know exactly. I had just got home when—"

"Yes, so it must have been close to six o'clock, perhaps a little after. Duffy's call for the police came in at twelve minutes before six. How long were you away from home?"

"I think I must have gone out about four." She thought back to the interview between Marcus and Jim; much had been said but the interview had been short. She said, "Yes, about that time— I'm not sure. I got home only a moment or two before Duffy and the policemen came."

Lieutenant Conti nodded. "I don't see why you should have to attend the inquest. Unless—oh, there might be a question about his state of mind."

"His—you mean suicide?"

"That's always a possibility," he said quietly.

She risked a question. "What will happen at the inquest?"

"Why, I should think there will be a verdict of accidental death. However, I'll be frank with you. Mr. Desart's first wife was murdered here, as you know. The case was never closed. So I was ordered to make very sure that the tragedy of yesterday was in fact an accident."

Careful. Oh, very careful, she thought. The corner of the terrace where Rose had been killed tugged at her senses as if a shadow had moved. Nothing was really safe. She said firmly, "I don't understand you."

His green eyes looked skeptical but he replied politely. "When a violent death occurs it is always our job as policemen to discover just what brought it about. Now this looks like accident. It could have been suicide. But there was once a murder here. Obviously, because of that murder, it's our duty to make sure that your husband's death was . . . well, not murder too."

"No! No, how could it have been!"

"I don't know—I couldn't possibly make a guess. But it is within the scope of possibility that your husband knew of some evidence concerning his first wife's murder, and that her murderer knew this. Did Mr. Desart have any special or, say, new evidence about his first wife's murder?"

"No! No, he couldn't have had!" She spoke too quickly; instantly it occurred to her that such a path of inquiry might lead the police away from any questions about Jim.

She'd forgotten the clear, cold light on the terrace. The lieutenant frowned a little, eying her. He said, "I'm afraid you've bruised your cheek, Mrs. Desart."

Lie, she told herself swiftly, lie. You must never let him know anything about the dreadful scene with Marcus because of Jim. She said, "Did I? I didn't know it."

His green eyes were rather narrow. "It must be painful, just below the eye. In fact, it looks as if both sides of your face were bruised."

"I didn't know—" She turned toward the house and saw the door into the gallery. "I must have stumbled against the door when the policemen ran in. I don't remember."

"Oh," said Lieutenant Conti. "Well now, I think I have a notion of what your husband did yesterday. You had callers about noon. I've talked to his law partner, Mr. Gould, and to his other friend, Douglas Woodard. Mrs. Minot was here. They told me that Senator Stidger from Mr. Desart's home state was here too. I understand that your husband had decided to make another attempt to run for the Senate. I gather that the four men lunched together to talk over the political situation. Later in the day Mr. Desart returned home."

"Yes, that's right."

"Did your husband seem quite as usual?"

This time it was strangely hard to lie, but she said, "Yes."

"I see. And then you went for a walk?"

"Yes. I had barely got home when—"

"Yes, I know." He turned from her and looked out over the hedge. The towers of the city rose all around them. Water tanks loomed up, solid and black; ventilators and chimneys stood out sharply against the gray sky; antennas on the roofs sprang out like spiders. Here and there were other little oases of green which would later become roof gardens. Lieutenant Conti said, "The exact time of his death is difficult to establish, but the doctor says it must have occurred within an hour of the time Duffy found him. Your maid said that the day before his death Mr. Desart climbed up on the wall and became dizzy, and that Mr. Woodard caught him before he fell."

"Yes. He had started to tie up the willow then. That one, you see it is tied now—"

"Yes, I see. I believe your maid said that she was in the living room, just at the door of the small elevator there, and saw the incident through that window. Was anyone else on the terrace at the time?"

"Woody and I were here. Nobody else."

The lieutenant crossed to the wrought-iron gate separating the terrace and a strip of roof which, blocked by the penthouse and for the most part out of sight, had its own water tanks and ventilators and antennae. He peered through the gate. "If anyone was out there, on that section of the roof, he could have seen through this gate," he said absently.

"I don't remember seeing anyone there. Besides, what difference could it make?"

"I don't know, really." He was standing at the corner of the terrace, and his neatly polished black shoes were planted firmly upon the nonexistent shadow. He turned, thanked her and, re-entering the apartment, ran down the stairs as easily as a very young man.

Sue went hurriedly to the dressing room and did what she could with make-up to hide the bruises on her cheeks. Then, closing her bedroom door, she telephoned Jim. He answered so promptly that she guessed that he had been waiting for her call.

"Jim, I'll try to meet you about three this afternoon."

"Where?"

"Somewhere near."

"The park at Sixty-first and Fifth."

"Yes." She hung up at once.

Common sense told her that her apprehensions had carried her too far along a dangerous path of reasoning. But common sense told her too that Jim's return and the scene with Marcus could easily provide the police with a motive for murder. So the important thing was an alibi for Jim during the time when Marcus must have fallen from the terrace. Until now the word alibi had been a word in newspapers, a word for a joking excuse.

There were many telephone calls; Belle took them all. Somehow it was decided that the services for Marcus would take place in his home state as soon as the police permitted it. Aubrey would see to all the arrangements, including plane tickets for Belle and Sue. Belle would see to their packing, and since Sue had no suitable black dress or coat, Belle offered to shop for her. She left after lunch.

When she had gone, and while Pauline was on the first floor of the apartment, Sue went down by way of the private elevator. It was close to three, a deserted hour in the lobby of the big apartment house. Aside from a porter putting some new light bulbs in a wall sconce, she saw nobody.

Jim was waiting at a bench beside the wall of the park. He was wearing civilian clothing again, a grayish tweed which looked new and fitted the lines of his tall figure far better than the old suit he had worn the first night she had seen him. He could have been any young man waiting for his girl, good-looking, tanned, his brown hair bleached by the sun. When he saw her his eyes lit up and he sprang up to meet her. It was like old times, like days of magic and happiness that were strangely far away.

She put out her hands and Jim took them. After a moment he said huskily, "We'd better walk. Can't stand here like idiots."

For the first time Sue thought to herself, Now there is nobody who can separate us. She must have realized it in her heart, her deepest thoughts must have considered it, but she had not let herself put it into words. Now it hovered in the air all around her, enclosing her with Jim. Nobody now could separate them. Except, said a cold little voice, the police. They could call Jim a suspect. "Jim," she cried. "Where were you when it happened?"

Jim took her arm and linked it within his own. He put his hand over hers. "Now take it easy. I may have been near the apartment house."

"Jim! Oh, no!"

"Now wait, Sue. After I left I walked downtown. I just kept on walking. Thinking. I stopped in the Plaza bar and had a couple of drinks. Finally I went back to your apartment. That was about five, I think, perhaps later."

"Why did you go back?"

"I didn't like the look in his eyes when I left," Jim said

flatly. "The more I thought of it the less I liked it. I decided that I'd been a fool to leave you with him. He looked dangerous, that's all. So I went back. Now wait—" Her hand had tightened, clutching his own. "The elevator man saw me, but I'd never seen him before—"

"He's a new man. He wouldn't have known you, but he'd remember your uniform."

"I'm not so sure," Jim said. "There was a fracas going on between two dogs and their owners, two women. A real squabble. The elevator man was trying to run the elevator and separate the dogs and—no, he may not remember. Anyway, I got off at your floor and rang and rang, but when nobody came to the door, I left again. This must have been after five. Going on six. When did Marcus—when do the police say it happened?"

"They're not sure," Sue said desolately. "But he was found a little before six. The police doctor said he must have fallen within the hour. Oh, Jim, and you were there!"

"He'd have answered the doorbell, wouldn't he? If he'd been alive then?"

"Oh, I don't know! The elevator man will remember your leaving. He's certain to remember that. He'll remember your uniform."

"It's a busy time. The buzzer kept ringing from the ground floor, and he really didn't seem to pay me any special attention. He was watching for the floor signals. There was a stack of evening papers in the elevator too, and he kept stopping to look at the names and deliver the papers."

"I hoped you'd have an alibi."

"Do the police suggest that it wasn't an accident? Tell me exactly what the police lieutenant said to you."

She told him, making sure that she omitted nothing. Jim walked on quietly, thinking it over. Finally he said, "In view of Rose's murder, yes. Naturally they'd ask themselves if this could be murder too. I didn't kill him, Sue—"

"I know that."

"—but I might have if— What happened to your face?"

"I hoped—I put on make-up—"

"That's what I was afraid of." Jim held her arm close to his side, and his voice was strange and cold. "So that's why you went for that long walk yesterday. You were afraid of him."

"Yes, in a way. I was furious too. But I knew he'd cool down, come to his senses."

"Why did you go back?"

"I had to."

"Yes—well—but I don't believe he'd have changed."

"He might have. Yesterday was the wrong time to talk to him. Did you go to his office?"

"I went down to Wall Street. Then it struck me that I ought to have an appointment—I didn't fancy sitting around, kicking my heels and waiting to see him. So I phoned, but his secretary said he hadn't been there that day."

"Did you give your name?"

"No, I thought I'd better see him and then tell him. So I had lunch, at Fraunces Tavern. I spent some time looking at the collection, examining their banners and all that, to give Marcus time to get to the office. But when I phoned again he still hadn't come in. That's when I went to your place and met him in the lobby. Why did you say that yesterday was the wrong time to talk to him?"

"He was upset. Aubrey Gould—that's his law partner—and Senator Stidger—he was elected after Marcus withdrew from his first campaign—came to talk him out of running for office."

As she told him of the talk which had so nearly ended

in a brawl, Jim listened attentively. "You don't suppose Senator Stidger pushed him over the wall," he said dryly when she had finished.

"Good heavens, no!"

"Sounds as if he had a reason to get rid of Marcus. What was it Marcus said about Senator Stidger's record?"

"He said that the Senator should take a look at his record, that Stidger had forced him to say this in the privacy of his own home and that he shouldn't force him to say it publicly."

"Sounds like a threat."

Marcus can be mean, Belle had said. Sue hadn't quite believed her.

They moved to one side to permit a cortege of perambulator, two children, two dogs and a harassed nursemaid to pass. Jim said, "I can't believe that Senator Stidger has any secret skeletons."

"He couldn't have forced Marcus up on the wall," Sue said. "Why, it had to be an accident! Marcus wouldn't climb up there and just stand still and let anybody push him over!"

An odd expression came into Jim's face. "It could be done if somebody had managed to hit him over the head first."

This deflated her. "How?"

"Easy enough, I should think, if anybody really wanted to. Don't look at me like that. I'm used to fighting no holds barred. What about this Aubrey fellow, his partner?"

"Aubrey Gould."

"Yes. He objected to Marcus' decision to enter politics again. Is he a big man, muscular?"

"Aubrey wouldn't murder anybody. He's a lawyer. He knows too much."

"He's known Marcus a long time?"

"Oh, yes. Their decision to form a partnership was the

main reason for Marcus' coming to New York to live. He rarely went home. He kept his house there and a small office, but that's all. The—the services are to be there. I'll be away for—I don't know how long. The time hasn't been decided yet."

They walked on for a moment and then Jim said, "Sue, let's get something straight. You don't believe that it was an accident."

"I don't know."

"Or suicide?"

"No. That is, it might have been, but—"

"You're afraid."

"Yes! Yes, I am. I'm afraid they'll say you killed him."

"Well, I didn't, so we've got to go on that basis. I think we should immediately tell the police—this Lieutenant Conti you mentioned—the whole thing."

"The whole—"

"Tell him that you married Marcus believing I had been killed. Tell him I returned, tell him I came to see you, tell him we talked to Marcus—"

"Jim! No! Can't you see—?"

"I do see. Further than you can just at this moment. This thing has happened; we can't just dismiss it, we've got to wade through it."

"People have been charged with murder—I mean innocent people—and found guilty and—"

"Not often. Please listen. We have our whole lives before us. You are free now. Marcus is no longer an obstacle. But there's still a barrier. I'd like to snatch you off to the marriage license bureau and the nearest preacher right now, but I'm not going to. I'm not going to—to touch you, not going to look at you if I can help it"—he laughed a little but he obviously meant what he said—"until this thing is completely cleared up. You can't live in the shadow of it."

He seemed to think that over, and added gravely, "And neither can I. We've got to go through with any sort of inquiry or suspicion or—or anything at all. For instance, right now someone is following us."

chapter 11

Sue had heard only the murmur of passing cars and the cries of children in the park.

"Don't look around," Jim said.

She stopped herself in the act of turning. "But nobody would follow us!"

"Somebody is doing it just the same. Possibly an emissary of your Lieutenant Conti. We'll turn around in a moment and go to meet him."

"I can't hear anybody. How do you know?"

"My sense of awareness has grown a little sharp recently. Sue, a number of people must already know that I came back and saw you. We *can't* keep it from the police!"

"Belle Minot knows or guesses about you," she admitted reluctantly.

"The pretty little lady who was there yesterday? I thought so. She looked like an extremely intelligent woman."

"But she likes me. She wouldn't do anything to hurt me. She won't tell anybody that you were there."

"I don't intend to keep my existence a complete secret. It's been kept out of the news for some reason—security, I suppose. Marcus had me all but apologizing for being alive yesterday and—"

"Belle will never tell anybody that you came to see me! Especially not the police!"

"But, Sue, I've told you, the police have ways of finding out things."

"I think Woody—Douglas Woodard—guessed who you were, but he'd never go out of his way to tell the police that an old friend of mine called on me. You had a perfect right to come to see me."

"Sue, you must believe me. There's no use in trying to keep my return a secret and no reason to try to. I didn't kill Marcus. We did have a motive for getting rid of him, but we didn't. Now let's turn around. Keep talking."

They wheeled. Perhaps twenty feet behind them a man was taking out a cigarette from a package. He wore a raincoat, a red tie and a rather battered hat. As he lit the cigarette, the flare of the match fell upon a nondescript face. She had never in her life seen him before. He stood still, fussing with the match, and as they passed him Jim said, "I'm glad Mrs. Minot is staying with you."

Sue heard herself replying, "She's a good friend."

Sue felt that the man had turned to watch them, and she had an odd impulse to quicken her steps. Jim held her to an easy stroll. He said, "Oh, I think I see a cab!" and waved at an approaching taxi.

"I'd rather walk," Sue began, but the taxi had swerved to the curb and halted.

Jim opened the door, shook hands with her in a friendly but formal way and said, "Think over what I've said."

"Jim, wait. How long did he follow us? Who was he?"

"I don't know. Don't worry about it." He closed the door of the taxi.

She gave her address to the driver because there was nothing else to do. As she glanced back through the window the nondescript man had reversed himself too, and was strolling along behind Jim. She could not believe that they were being followed by a detective, but Jim's return was a motive for murder and Lieutenant Conti had impressed her as an able and thorough man. Jim was wrong to want to tell him anything! When Jim had told her to think over what he'd said, he must have meant that he would say nothing without her consent. She took what reassurance she could from that.

When they reached the main door of the apartment house, old Polk came hurrying out on his big flat feet to open the door for her. As he helped her out solicitously he said, "I'm so sorry. I was terribly shocked."

Polk knew that Jim had returned and that he had come to see her the night before Marcus was murdered. She had a swift impulse to ask the old man to keep the visit a secret, but she knew Jim would have disapproved. She said only, "Thank you, Polk."

His big kind face was troubled and his bleary eyes looked as if they held tears. He escorted her over the curb as if she were a thousand years old—and I feel it, she thought—and into the lobby. "You have some callers," he said. "Mrs. Minot is here. Mr. Woodard came and Mr. Gould."

"Thank you, Polk."

As the door of the private elevator opened she heard Belle saying, "I think you've done very well, Aubrey. And Woody, too. I'm sure that Sue will agree."

When she entered the living room Woody sprang up. Aubrey rose too, with his air of youthfulness, and contrived to kiss her hand gallantly. Belle smiled. "There you are, my dear. I'm glad you got some fresh air. Everything is arranged. The service is to be tomorrow. It seems there has to be an inquest, but it's to be postponed. New York is such a big city," she said vaguely, "so many things for public officials to see to all the time. Accidents, homicides—that is"—she caught herself up shortly—"I mean there's no hurry about it, and Aubrey and Woody say that the only possible verdict is accidental death, anyway—that is, unless somebody hints at suicide—"

"Nobody would do that," Aubrey said. "Marcus was respected. Nobody would cast a slur upon his memory."

"No, certainly not," Belle said smoothly, as if she and Sue had never so much as questioned the manner of Marcus' death.

Sue said blankly, "Tomorrow?"

Belle said quickly, "It's all arranged. The police have permitted—they have released the body, I mean—we take the night plane. The services will be tomorrow morning. Aubrey is going with us. He and Woody have phoned, and —everything is arranged, and I got the black dress and coat and hat for you. Some black gloves and a veil, too. Pauline has already packed for you. We'll stay only for the day and take the plane back tomorrow night. Then you're to come to my apartment and stay with me as long as you want to."

The three of them took the night plane; Woody drove them to the airport. On arrival they were met by a group of soft-voiced, sympathetic men and taken to a modern, sparkling hotel. The services were at ten in the morning; the big church was packed. Sue knew no one except Senator Stidger, whom she had not expected to see; he looked pale and troubled, shook hands with her, then went hurriedly back to the airport and Washington. Many people shook her hand; and all of them were kind to, if a little curious about, this young woman who had been Marcus' wife so briefly. Belle constantly beside her gave Sue a support which she had not realized how much she needed. There was also a short burial service beside a stone marked "Rose Desart, wife of Marcus Desart," and it seemed fitting to Sue that her husband would lie beside the woman he had truly loved.

Afterward someone took them to an enormous, comfortable house, where they were given sherry and sandwiches and people talked to her some more and said the same kind things. Throughout the day she felt as if she were an onlooker. Then it was over at last and they were on the evening plane.

"I didn't think you'd want to see his house," Belle said worriedly. "It's a dreary old place. Besides, it's all closed up, and–"

"No, I wouldn't want to see it," she replied. It had never been her home; she had never once thought of it as a place where they might live one day.

She wondered how many of those sympathetic and low-voiced people had known the Marcus she had glimpsed twice. There had been nothing but praise for him, nothing but friendship and regret. That was natural, though, to be expected. And clearly that good side of Marcus was one to be remembered.

She wondered too, listening to the beat of the engines, if

any of those old friends of Marcus were speculating about his death. Was it suicide? Or was it conceivably murder? None of them would have forgotten that Rose had been murdered. She was almost sure that Aubrey was wondering, but his face was bland and unquestioning.

Woody also gave not the slightest indication that he had any doubt as to how Marcus had died. He met them at the airport with a rented car and chauffeur. As they got into the long limousine, Sue thought that there was something familiar about a man sitting well back in a car parked behind the limousine. They were almost at Belle's apartment before it occurred to her that he looked like Lieutenant Conti.

All at once she was sure that it *was* Lieutenant Conti. She was suddenly sure that the man in the red tie, strolling behind her and Jim near the Park, had in fact been a detective. So that alone, she thought dismally, meant that the police were still not satisfied about Marcus' death. After that, wherever she went, she watched for a watcher; sometimes she thought that she had discovered one, but she was never sure.

She could not talk to Jim for three days more. From the moment they arrived at Belle's apartment, the older woman exercised a friendly but dogged surveillance. The apartment was in the East Sixties, only a few streets from Marcus' apartment; yet Belle made it almost impossible for her guest to visit the penthouse, no matter what excuse she used. If Sue said there might be messages, Belle telephoned and talked to Pauline; if Pauline happened to be out, she would then say that there was nothing urgent. If Sue invented a need for aspirin or toothpaste, thinking of using a telephone booth in the drugstore, Belle went with her. If she took a walk, Belle took a walk, too. There was never a moment when Belle was not within hearing distance; yet it was done so affectionately and so subtly that there was nothing Sue could say or do.

But Belle never mentioned suicide, much less murder. She only firmly guarded Sue.

Lieutenant Conti did not turn up at all, yet Sue expected him whenever the doorbell rang. Though she had an uneasy sense of his tenacious observance from somewhere, she told herself that she must be wrong. She couldn't guess what Jim was doing, but in the long nights she thought of him. Perhaps he had been right when he said that they must keep "hands off" until the tragic question of Marcus' death was fully answered. She agreed also that a period of time should pass out of respect to Marcus, though a long wait would be merely hypocritical. But that decision could wait. What she could not agree with was Jim's belief that Conti should be told everything about his return and his interview with Marcus. She turned cold whenever she thought of it, and she prayed that Jim would observe his implied promise to say or do nothing without her approval. If only she could be sure!

The day after their return to New York, Aubrey brought over a copy of Marcus' will. He was clearly prepared to read it word for word, for he had a certain flair for the dramatic. Belle put an end to that, so he told her and Belle only its main provisions.

First there were some small bequests: a thousand dollars to Pauline, a thousand dollars to Jean Wilson.

Belle said, "Jean Wilson—" and stopped.

Aubrey fiddled with the papers in his hands. "His former secretary. Shall I go on?"

There were a few not so small bequests to charities; Sue began to see that Marcus had been a very rich man. There was a large bequest to Woody: fifty thousand dollars, as well as anything personal which Woody wished.

Then Aubrey cleared his throat. "There's also a large bequest to me—another fifty thousand dollars. I am only one of three executors. An executor is not usually a legatee, but in this case Marcus insisted because of losses to the firm in the event of his death."

He looked at Sue, who said, "That seems quite right. You were his partner."

Aubrey looked relieved. "The bequest actually goes to the firm, so to speak. You understand, I hope, that we'll have an outside firm of accountants do an audit so that Marcus' entire share will go to his estate. This will take some time; these things always do. Obviously"—he hesitated—"the partnership is at an end."

Sue supposed he was addressing her again and said, "Why, yes, of course."

Aubrey flipped pages nervously again. "Well, as a matter of fact, I was speaking to Belle—that is, to both of you. That is—"

Belle sat up straight. "For heaven's sake, Aubrey, what are you maundering about?"

Aubrey brought out a fine monogrammed handkerchief. "He meant to change his will, I'm sure, after his marriage. But the fact is that he didn't change it. His will was made shortly after Rose's death and it leaves the entire remainder of his estate to Belle."

There was a long pause. Belle didn't say a word. Aubrey carefully didn't look at Sue.

She said, "But that's all right. Belle was his family. We were married a very short time. I didn't think of—I didn't expect anything."

Aubrey shook his head. "My dear Sue! Well, fortunately,

there's a law to protect wives—I should say widows. You're entitled to a third of his estate, and a very substantial estate it is. Yesterday I saw his home bankers and the young man, Stanson, who runs his office there. I've also talked to his New York bankers and his brokers. It's a very good portfolio, I must say. A fine estate, even"—he winced and all but groaned—"even after inheritance taxes."

Belle cut in icily. "I'll not take one penny of Marcus' money."

"Belle!" Aubrey's pale eyes were startled. "Money is money!"

"I'm not saying anything about money. Everybody cares about money. If anybody says he doesn't, be careful, for he'll take the gold fillings out of your teeth before you can say wink. But I won't take Marcus' money."

Belle's pretty face was suddenly not pretty; it was like stone, hard and implacable, and her eyes were angry.

Aubrey put away his fine handkerchief, tapped his glistening fingernails on the table beside him and finally said after a long pause, "You'll have to take it, Belle, and pay the taxes, even if you give it away later. And you can only give it away to certain—well, you can give some to Sue but not much that's tax free, and the rest of it—"

Belle's usually charming voice was sharp and cold. "See to it that I give Sue as much as I can at once, Aubrey. And in the meantime, make a new will for me, leaving every single thing I have to Sue. I want that done and signed today."

"But, really, Belle, this takes time—"

"Today," Belle said implacably.

"Dear me," Aubrey said after a thoughtful pause, "you might be a very rich woman some day, Sue. That is—" He caught himself and glanced at Belle, who said tartly, "I feel in very good health, Aubrey."

"Of course, yes, I didn't mean— Dear me, I must hurry. I'll leave this copy of Marcus' will here for you to look over at your leisure. Oh, yes, I'll see to the tax appraisers. His safe-deposit vault and his office safe and desk will have to be opened in their presence. I'll see to all that. The other two executors are young Stanson and the president of his bank at home. He spoke to you yesterday, Sue, but I expect you didn't know his name. However, if you wish to talk to him or to Stanson—"

"My will," Belle said. "This afternoon."

chapter 12

The will came that afternoon, brought by a young man from the office who looked with covert interest at them. As Belle read it carefully, Sue asked her, timidly in the face of Belle's look of stony determination, whether she had other relatives or close friends. But Belle cut her short. "This is what I want. Now then, my signature has to be witnessed. You'll do, for one." She looked at the young man so sternly that he wriggled in his chair. "Call Ella, will you, Sue?"

Ella was an elderly maid who, to Sue's astonishment, actually wore a cap. It was a bare ruffle of white, usually perched on one side, but still it was a cap and like a tiny footnote to history. Ella appeared, and in a moment two copies of the will were signed, witnessed and tucked away in a large envelope in the young man's briefcase. "Tell Mr.

Gould to see to it," Belle said. "Thank you. Good afternoon."

The young man seemed glad to escape.

Belle was curt and snappish all that evening, and indeed all the next day, but she remained a tenacious watchdog.

The next two days seemed an oddly blank passage of time. Sue could only go over and over the same circles of conjecture which arrived nowhere. It was like walking through a trackless country which had no landmarks, no points of either departure or arrival. She played gin with Belle; she went with her for a long walk and wrongly suspected of surveillance a little man in a red tie who after three blocks shot mysteriously out of sight into a cross street and a few blocks later appeared again, not so mysteriously, towed at the end of a leash by a large and athletic German shepherd. They whirled around a corner and were not seen again.

The next morning she packed her suitcase before breakfast and over coffee thanked Belle and told her she was going home.

Belle sighed. "You'll have to go sometime, I suppose. There's something I must tell you." She found it hard to say, though. She crumbled up some toast, bit her pretty lip and finally said, "I talked to your young man. Jim Locke."

"When? What did he say?"

"He phoned here. He had phoned your place and Pauline told him that you were here. I didn't call you; I thought it best to talk to him myself. I told him to leave. Go home, go somewhere, but leave for the present. He agrees with me, though not for the same reasons," she added rather shortly. "Oh, he told me that he had talked to you and roughly what he had said. He's right, of course. I like your young man, Sue, but my reason for telling you not to see him is simply prudence. I know something about police investigation. I do not believe that the police are sure that Marcus' death was an accident. Neither do you."

"What else did Jim say?"

"Only that he had to be away for a few days. Now, Sue, I know you've thought that now you are free and that Jim is waiting and—"

"I couldn't have helped thinking about it, but that doesn't mean I wanted Marcus' death. I would never have wanted that."

"But you have thought, Now I'm free. You've got to stop thinking anything like that. Don't let anybody in the world guess that such a thought has ever occurred to you. Now, about this money that Marcus left me. Aubrey will see to it that you get your legal share as soon as it can be done. Marcus left a very large fortune, as you know. I wish he hadn't left it all to me."

"He loved you—"

Belle lifted opaque brown eyes to Sue. "Suppose that was conscience money."

"Conscience—" Sue waited a moment, then leaned across the table. "Belle, he didn't—he wouldn't have killed Rose! He loved her."

So that accounted for the change in Belle when Aubrey had told her of Marcus' will. Belle said, "I told you that sometimes I thought that perhaps, just perhaps, Marcus and Rose had had a terrible quarrel and that he had lost his head and then been sorry. I told you then that I was wrong. Yet all that money to me!"

Sue herself had accused Marcus of killing Rose in a moment of shock at his sudden brutality. But she had spoken in stunned anger. She said slowly, "You're not being logical. If you think, I mean only suspect, that Marcus killed Rose—"

"Nobody can stop the things that come into one's mind. You don't understand; there are two points of view. I'm telling you what occurred to *me* when I heard that Marcus had left his money to me. That's one point of view—*mine*—and it's only a notion. But another point of view is that of the police. That's what *you* must keep in mind—all the time, every minute."

"But, Belle, if Marcus had killed Rose, who would have—?"

Belle broke in. "Who would have murdered him? I don't know. Aubrey has thought of murder. So has Woody."

"Did they say so?"

"I can tell. The bruise on your cheek is quite healed now."

"Is that why you've kept me here?"

"I didn't want you to rush out and see Jim and do something foolish. But, yes, I wanted that bruise to heal. Somebody might get ideas."

"I think Lieutenant Conti already has an idea," Sue said soberly. "He asked me about it. I told him I ran into the door."

"Good heavens, couldn't you think of something better than that! Your veil concealed it at the service, and now it's quite gone." Belle sipped some coffee, which must have been stone-cold. "Now then, remember that time helps. I've seen something of the world. Believe me, it's not really what you do or don't do that counts as much as what people *think* you do or don't do. That sounds cynical, but keep it in mind. Keep on wearing black. Get yourself some more dresses. And don't, I beg of you, don't see this young man of yours for a long time. I didn't like that police lieutenant who came around to see you. He talked to me too—about nothing, really, but still it was too much. He tried to get a complete picture of your life with Marcus. I wasn't born yesterday," she said tiredly. "He got nothing out of me. And nothing at all about Jim Locke. But be careful, my dear."

At the door she kissed Sue and told her to come to see her or to telephone her at any time.

It was a pleasant April day, with a blue sky and fleecy white clouds. Leaves were coming out on the trees along the avenue. When Sue reached the familiar entrance of the apartment building no one was at the door. Since the main elevator was at the third floor ascending, she groped into her handbag for the key and unlocked the door to the private elevator.

Pauline had been alone in the penthouse all this time. She suspected that the maid had spent most of her time at one moving picture or another, for quite obviously the small elevator had not been dusted and cleaned. The mirror over the table looked slightly dull. A brown leaf lay in a corner; idly she picked it up; it was a geranium leaf, withered and dried. She was still holding it when she opened the door and went into the living room, and she dropped it in an ashtray. Strangely, the room seemed slightly different, but she couldn't have said why.

As soon as she entered her bedroom, however, she knew why. The same cushions were on the chaise longue, but in a slightly different arrangement. Some of the ashtrays, the photograph of her father in its silver frame, the books, the various small objects which take up a certain place and stay there without moving an inch, seemed now to be in subtly different positions. She was seized with a monstrous and frightening notion: the room, perhaps the whole house, had been thoroughly searched during her absence.

The evidence was all too clear that the police were still interested in Marcus' death.

Something cold and hard came into her throat. She went to the stairs and called down to Pauline, who came pattering through the dining room, and appeared, her puff of hair disheveled, at the bottom.

"Madame! I didn't expect you!"

"Pauline, who has been in the house?"

"Who? But nobody, madame! There were telephone calls—I have a list. But nobody has been here! Of course, as Madame may know, I have been out a few times. I knew that Madame would not object."

"How often? How long at a time?"

"Well, but . . . Oh, naturally I went to the cinema sometimes. Is anything wrong? I saw to the house, madame." Pauline began to rally. "Naturally I knew that Madame wouldn't wish me to stay alone all the time here. It was not pleasant, you understand, especially at night. Two tragedies."

It was perhaps then that Sue began to sense a slight change in Pauline. It was nothing she could analyze, but she did have an impression of a kind of furtiveness in Pauline's manner. She was as eagerly inquisitive as always, perhaps even more so, yet it struck Sue that this woman too might have been wondering just how Marcus died. She said, "You won't be alone now. I've come home until—well, until things—"

"Madame, if you are thinking of changing your residence, I hope you will give me a good reference."

"Yes. Yes, of course. I'll let you know when—if I have any plans."

She turned back, crossed the gallery and glanced out. The pink flowers were thriving. Then she remembered the shabby little candy box, tied up with a string, holding letters from Jim, the telegram from his mother telling her of his presumed death and her diamond ring. The box told the whole story. She ran to her room, kneeled down and jerked open the drawer of the small French chest. The box with all its revealing contents was gone.

No matter what Belle had said, she had to talk to Jim. But when she called Jim's club she was told that Commander Locke had left. He had left no address; no, he was not expected back; no, there was no information as to his present whereabouts.

As she put down the telephone Pauline's high heels came tapping across the living-room floor. "Mr. Woodard is here," she told Sue. She had combed her mound of black hair. "Shall I show him up, madame?"

She met Woody in the living room. He took her hands, bent over unexpectedly and kissed her. "Dear Sue. It's been a bad time. But it's all in the past now, remember that!"

"I'm not sure it's in the past. Isn't there such a thing as a search warrant?"

He understood at once. "The police have been here while you were away?"

"They took something. A box. I want it back. They had no right—"

"They had no right to take anything. They had no right to search without a search warrant."

"I want that box back."

"All right. Let me think a moment. If they had no search warrant—"

But when questioned, Pauline, shaking her head emphatically, said that she had seen no police and didn't know what a search warrant was.

"All right," Woody said. "All right." He dismissed Pauline with such a definite nod that she almost scurried down the stairs. Taking Sue's hand, he drew her to the sofa. "What about this box?"

"It's an old candy box, tied with a string."

"I take it that there are things in it which—forgive me if I'm brutal, but I've got to be—there are things in it which are connected with this young man, this Navy flier who returned from Vietnam. Is that right?"

As her mind raced, Woody said, "Marcus mentioned him months ago. When he told me that you and he were going to be married, he told me that the man you had intended to marry had been killed in Vietnam. So when I met Locke here I remembered. You see, if the police have any idea that Marcus' death might, just might, not have been an accident—I've got to say it—murder—then Jim Locke . . . I mean his return would supply a strong motive for murder."

So Belle was right. Woody and almost certainly Aubrey had thought of murder.

Woody turned her hand in his own, and looking at her palm as if to examine every little line, said, "Marcus was not the kind of man to let you go. I knew Marcus." He paused a moment and then said, "I was one of Marcus' best friends. I admired him; I had reason to be grateful to him. But he was hard. He had his likes and dislikes. He hated Stidger, for example. I think he decided to try to run for office again mainly because he hated Stidger."

Jim had suggested, merely as a possibility, that Senator Stidger had a motive for getting rid of Marcus. She said, "Why did Marcus hate Senator Stidger? What did he have against him?"

"I think, actually, it was because they were so different. Marcus was—oh, we loved him, Sue, but we have to admit that he was naturally dramatic. He had a flair for public speaking; he loved an audience. Stidger is the opposite; he's quiet, self-effacing. But that threat of Marcus' about disclosing something or other couldn't really have been valid. Stidger has a perfectly clear public record. He was elected with a big majority and he's trusted and respected. Of course—" Woody hesitated. "There are always some people in public life who wouldn't want every single act publicized to the world. But I can't see Stidger doing anything at all questionable. Of course, I don't really know him. Aubrey does, and certainly he got Stidger back here in a hurry when Marcus decided to try again for office. But that's not the point now. Where is this man Locke? I hope you're not seeing him, not just yet."

"He's not in town. I don't know where he is."

He gave her hand a brisk pat and released it. "You must remember that Marcus was well known. Anything you do is likely to be seen and commented upon. You must remember that while murder is unlikely, it is something the police have to consider. You've thought of it, I'm sure. And because Rose was murdered, it's probable that the police are trying to find some connection between her murder and Marcus' death."

"There couldn't be a—a blood feud, some fantastic thing like that? Somebody who hated both Rose and Marcus? Perhaps someone from his home whom they knew?"

"I can't believe that. Oh, no! I was thinking that the police might believe that Marcus had got hold of some evidence about Rose's murderer, that the murderer found out, was scared and—and pushed Marcus off that wall."

"Conti said something like that."

"So they are considering it!"

"But he said it was an accident."

The telephone rang and she sprang up. "It may be Jim." She ran into the bedroom and he followed her slowly, pausing in the doorway. She took down the telephone. "Yes, hello—"

A strange voice, a rough voice, said, "Mrs. Desart. I want to talk to Mrs. Desart."

"This is Mrs. Desart."

There was a pause, then the voice said so clearly that she couldn't have mistaken the words, "Is there a reward?"

"A *what*?"

"A reward. I told you. Reward."

chapter 13

"Reward! But what—who . . . You must have the wrong number!"

"No, wait, lady. Are you really Mrs. Desart?"

"I'm Mrs. Desart. I don't know what you're talking about. There's no reward for—for anything."

Something was thudding hard in Sue's throat, as if her heart had jumped up and interfered with her breathing. Woody was running across the room. Suddenly the voice said, "Oh, there'll be a reward. I saw a lot. You think it over, lady—"

Woody took the receiver. A babble of sounds came from it, and he listened, his face intent but puzzled. Then Sue heard the click as the other telephone was put down.

Frowning, Woody hung up. "I couldn't make any sense out of it. I heard you say reward. What was it?"

"He wanted to know about a reward. He said I was to think it over. What did he mean?"

"I don't think he meant anything," Woody said slowly. "He sounded drunk to me. I could tell you were frightened. Well, forget it. It was only some sick fool who gets a kick out of phoning like that. No way to trace him."

"Reward," she said. "It's as if he thought he knew something about Marcus' death. I don't see what else he could mean."

"He didn't mean that," Woody said firmly. "He was too drunk to mean anything. Perhaps you'd better have a private number, though. All the stories in the papers have brought Marcus' name and yours into prominence. I'll see to it if you want me to."

She thought about Jim, who might telephone her. "No, no. It was nothing, of course. Besides, Pauline usually takes the phone calls and she always asks for names."

"You want to talk to Jim Locke if he phones you. Well, I suppose I can't stop you. Now then, Aubrey is seeing to Marcus' will, as you know. If there's anything you want me to do, just let me know."

"Thank you, Woody. There are all of Marcus' . . . what the will calls personal effects. Aubrey says you're to have what you want."

"He told me about the money Marcus left me too. I didn't expect anything like that. It was very good of Marcus, very —like him. Well . . ." He said good-bye too quickly, as if he did not want to show any emotion.

She felt heartened by his visit; yet the penthouse seemed rather empty after he had gone, in spite of Pauline's presence downstairs. But she was reminded of the inevitable chore of putting Marcus' room in order, sorting things out, the clothing to be given to charity, odds and ends to be cleaned up. She went into his room to begin work.

By nature Marcus had been very orderly. He'd had little jewelry. She opened the leather box with its gold initials; she had never seen him wear the black-pearl studs which lay wedged in velvet. Probably the inheritance-tax appraisers would have to see these.

Pauline came to the door, eyed her and said, "Ah, so sad. The policeman is here again."

Sue was now eager to talk to Lieutenant Conti. He must have taken the box full of her memories and mementos of Jim. She went out into the living room, her head high, prepared for anything. But just then it struck her that there had been not the slightest sign of a search in Marcus' room. Nothing had been as much as an inch out of place.

Lieutenant Conti looked cool and self-possessed; his green eyes were kind but observant. In a curious way it was almost a relief to see him, as if the tiger that had been stealthily stalking her through the jungle had at last let itself be glimpsed. "I'm sorry to trouble you," he said again; it seemed to be his opening phrase.

She asked him to sit down as Pauline scurried off down the stairs without leaving her ears behind her. Somehow or other, Lieutenant Conti must have put the fear of God into her.

"I'm really sorry," Lieutenant Conti said, settling himself in Marcus' big green chair. "You see, some details have come up. I'm trying to fill in the picture of the afternoon your husband died. It seems that a Navy officer, Commander Locke, met your husband in the lobby and came up in your private elevator with him." He didn't even wait for her reply.

"I also understand that the commander called to see you the night before your husband's"—there was the slightest pause before Lieutenant Conti finished his sentence—"death."

He waited then, but as she said nothing he went on. "The

doorman, Polk, brought Locke up to the apartment. Polk didn't tell me until he had to, but the elevator man who took your friend down again told me all about it. It seems Polk sent him on some errand and smuggled—I beg your pardon, that is not the word— In any event, Polk himself brought the commander up here to your apartment. Your maid, Pauline, tells me that she heard him leave."

So it wasn't the fear of God or even fear of the police that had sent Pauline scurrying downstairs; it was fear of Sue.

The lieutenant said, "I've made some inquiries, Mrs. Desart. I understand that you were engaged to marry this man Locke, that he was reported killed in Vietnam, and that after some fifteen months he escaped and returned and came to see you."

Sue spoke at last, angrily. "You took the box! You read the letters. You saw my ring. You had no search warrant. That's not legal."

"What box?"

Sue rushed on before she quite took in what he had said. "The candy box! It had Jim's letters and my ring and some other things. You searched the place, you came into my house without a search warrant, I suppose Duffy let you in, yes, Duffy has a key, he must have let you in and you searched and took that box and—"

She stopped, for suddenly Lieutenant Conti had an air of alert wariness. Even his red hair seemed to lie quietly; his green eyes had sparks in them, but he didn't move a muscle except when he spoke. "Nobody from the police has entered your apartment. I have never seen or heard of this box you speak of. You'd better tell me all about it, Mrs. Desart."

"But it's gone! And somebody's been here. I can tell. If it wasn't the police, who was it?"

"It wasn't the police. We don't work like that. For one thing, you're quite right, we would have to have a search warrant. Who would be interested in this box you speak of?"

"Nobody! Nobody but the police!"

"You say there were letters from Commander Locke in it?"

"Yes."

"And the man you had intended to marry came back from the dead, in a manner of speaking. Why did he come to see Mr. Desart that afternoon?"

She wished that Woody or even pompous Aubrey were with her. "He . . . he came to see both of us. I think that would be expected."

At this evasiveness an oddly weary look came into Lieutenant Conti's green eyes. "I see that I'll have to talk to Commander Locke."

"He's not in town," she said without thinking.

"Oh, I know that," Lieutenant Conti said pleasantly. "He's at Bethesda Naval Hospital. They made him go down there for a final checkup. He'll be finished tomorrow."

She was so stunned that she didn't even ask how he had learned that, but he told her anyway. "It was easy to discover his club. When I inquired there they told me. It was simple."

The voice at the club switchboard had refused to tell *her* where Jim had gone, but of course a police inquiry was designed to elicit all sorts of facts.

Lieutenant Conti said, "If you do find out what happened to this candy box, I'll be glad if you'll let me know."

"I have no idea. It's been in a drawer in my bedroom. There was nothing of value. I mean, there was the diamond ring, but it was—well, Jim didn't have much money—"

"I see," said the lieutenant. "By the way, was any delivery made at this apartment the day your husband"—again there was the little pause—"died?"

"Delivery? Why, I suppose groceries—"

"No, no. I mean from a department store, tailors, anything like that?"

"I don't remember anything. Perhaps Pauline—"

"I've already talked to her," he said pleasantly. "She says there was no delivery of any kind. It's odd." He looked at her for a moment, his green eyes very clear and bright. "You see, there's a new elevator man on your elevator."

"Yes. I don't know his name."

"It's Orrington Allerdyce."

"Orrington—" She stopped.

There was the barest flicker of a grin on Conti's face, but he said only, "He tells me that they call him Orry. He says that he doesn't know the faces of the people here yet, or, which is important in this instance, their usual visitors. But he tells me that he took a man in blue uniform upstairs and then down that afternoon. It seems that there was a rather enthusiastic dogfight going on in the elevator as the visitor arrived. He didn't get a very good look at him, but the man was on the eleventh floor only a few minutes." Conti said this gently, as if to concede that Jim's stay on the eleventh floor could not have been long enough to murder a man.

Sue thought dismally of all the people in a big apartment house, all the watchers, all the eyes recording, not maliciously but merely observing. She wouldn't admit that Jim had told her about his second visit. She said, "What time was that?"

"Apparently it was after you had gone out for that long walk of yours. Evidently he rang your doorbell but nobody answered, for he came down again in only a moment or two. Orry thinks he might be able to identify him, but he's not at all sure. The trouble is that he—or at least a man in a blue uniform—had turned up earlier. Orry saw him. Sometime before—perhaps half an hour, Orry can't be sure—he came with a big box, like a dress box from some store. He carried it over his shoulder, Orry said, but not as if it were heavy. But Orry couldn't see his face owing to the box. He seemed to be looking over the lobby, but then somebody rang for the elevator, so Orry had to go up. When he got back to the lobby the man was gone. Now, maybe he was delivering something and simply got the wrong apartment house. I've talked to every tenant, or at least their maids, in the apartment house. Took quite a while. Don't be upset, I said I was investigating a delivery theft. The point is that nobody in the whole place had anything like a dress or a suit delivered that day. Now, did you permit anybody to come upstairs in this private elevator?"

"No!"

"I see." Lieutenant Conti thought for a moment, then thanked her and went across the gallery and down the stairs. Like Jim, he didn't hesitate.

The whole truth about Jim's visits to the penthouse was as good as out now. She might have known that no such secret could have been kept, not in a big apartment house with doormen and elevator men, even in spite of dog fights or distractions. But at least Conti had admitted that Jim couldn't have stayed long on the eleventh floor; that was something. He clearly suspected, though, that Jim had come earlier and that she had either given him a key to the private elevator, or come down in it herself and taken him up with her. He couldn't prove that, she told herself, and it hadn't happened. But the way Conti had of investigating every tiny event in the entire apartment house during the afternoon of Marcus' death—even a delivery man who had got the wrong address—was chilling.

The door to the private elevator slid open and Pauline came in. She couldn't have heard through that door, or could she? Sue said, "Pauline, I understand that you told Lieutenant Conti of Commander Locke's call the night before Mr. Desart's death?"

Pauline had not expected a direct accusation. She blinked and put a hand to her black, black hair. "But, madame, it is no secret. Everybody in the apartment house knows of his miraculous return after being reported dead. Everybody."

"Everybody! What do you mean?"

Pauline was now quite self-possessed, "But, madame, you have lived here so long. Everyone knew of your engagement to the young man. The maids in the other apartments, the butler in Mr. Melson's apartment, the elevator men, the doormen, the—why, even the laundresses. Most of these people have worked here for many years. Certainly they knew of it. And when Commander Locke went away the night he called here, someone saw him and told everybody else. You must see, madame, the interest in his return, the romance—"

"I see," Sue said dully. Of course they knew her; an army of employees ran the apartment house. Naturally, they talked of what went on; it was human nature. Again she felt as if a hundred eyes had been watching everything she did. She said, "What is it you want, Pauline?"

"I use the elevator because my feet hurt. The stairs!" Pauline said with the air of one referring to an old grievance, as indeed it was. "The window washer wants to see you."

"The window washer! Haven't I paid their bill?"

"Oh, madame, the bill comes from the office. No, this window washer asks to see *you*."

"But I don't understand—oh, tell him I'm busy, Pauline."

"Madame, forgive me. I think you must see him."

"Why on earth, Pauline? What are you talking about?"

"This window washer is—is serious."

She meant the word serious in its French connotation, meaning something very important indeed.

"Oh, all right. But tell him I'm busy and can take only a moment."

"Yes, madame."

Sue thought distractedly about window-washing. She was sure that she had paid the last bill, and as Pauline had said, the bills came from one of the offices employing the armies of men who, equipped with seat belts and squeegees, swarmed like intent, brave flies up and down the towering walls and windows of New York. Window-washing was one of the little penalties of living in a penthouse; somehow the windows became grimy sooner than those on the lower floors.

Pauline reappeared with a little grayish, baldish, wrinkled man in work clothes, motioned him toward Sue and then took the elevator down again.

The little man shifted from one shabbily clad foot to another and said rather hoarsely, "I've come about the reward."

The word reward was enough, but she recognized his voice too. "You phoned me!"

He nodded; he had a scraggly gray mustache and lines in his face. "I read the papers. They say it was an accident. It wasn't an accident. I saw it."

"You saw—"

He came a step or two nearer. "I saw it all. I saw the Navy man planting all those little flowers. Then I saw them talk. Then I saw him push him over the terrace."

Somehow she spoke. "I don't believe you."

He grinned a little. His eyes were bleary and faded but determined. "Oh, I saw it. I was on the roof over there—"

He nodded toward the windows. "I was washing windows. I was nearly ready to stop, it was close to five, but I felt a little sick and I went on up to the roof and smoked and looked around. I sat there on a bench for a long time, I don't know how long. It was getting dark, but I could see this terrace. I saw him plant the flowers, and I thought it was funny. So like Americans. If I had flowers my old woman would plant them—if I had a terrace. He'd just finished planting when the old man came out. They talked and—I didn't see it all, I had turned away to look at something else. When I turned back, it was just in time. He pushed him right over the edge of the terrace, and he fell and it made me very sick. And then I read the papers and they said it was an accident. I want a reward."

"You couldn't have seen—"

The little man's mustache curled up as if it hid a smile. "Oh, now, Mrs. Desart. It was the young commander. Everybody knows the story. He came back. I saw him push your husband over. Now then, my reward."

She backed away from him. She couldn't swallow and her mouth was dry. She made herself look at him.

A curious, half-shamed look came into his faded eyes. "It's too bad. A young couple like you. I'd hate to see them send him off to the penitentiary for the rest of his life. But I have to think of myself too. I'm a poor man. I make my living hanging out of people's windows. Sometimes," he said thoughtfully, "I see some odd things, but I've never seen anything like that. I think that first he hit the old man —I mean Mr. Desart—and then pitched him over. It made me sick. But then—well, he was very rich and you're his wife—his widow—and I'm a poor man, and this Navy flyer—"

"Stop!" She felt as if she were suffocating, and she forced herself to say slowly and carefully, "I've got to have time."

"Oh, I understand that. Sure, you can have time. Think

it over. A murder case is never closed until the murderer is convicted, I know that. There's time. But not too much time, you understand. I'm a poor man."

She made herself cross to the elevator and ring for it. She waited until it stopped at the door. Then she said, "Please go." She said it more emphatically, more angrily than she should have permitted herself to speak. The little man's faded eyes looked at her sullenly, but he nodded slowly and disappeared into the elevator.

She stood listening until she was sure he had gone. Then she sank down on the sofa. She ought to telephone Lieutenant Conti at once; that was the sensible thing to do. But this was a dangerous story, and this was a dangerous witness.

chapter 14

Perhaps the window washer had made it up; perhaps he wasn't a witness to anything. Yet when he had said that he had seen Marcus fall and that he had felt sick, she had believed him.

But he must have invented the rest of it—the man in the blue uniform thrusting Marcus over the parapet. The whole story of Jim's return apparently was known by everybody in the apartment house, and all of them had talked. The little man had heard about it and about her marriage to Marcus; one of the porters, anybody, could have told him. So he had thought of blackmail.

She went to the telephone, determined to take the sensible course and talk to Lieutenant Conti. But though she began to dial, her hand stopped; she found it impossible to repeat this altogether too circumstantial story to the police. Jim had not been on the terrace at all; his only talk with Marcus had taken place in the living room. When he had returned to the house no one had answered his ring, and he had gone away again. Orry corroborated this. But the window washer's story was too much of a threat. There was nothing she could do.

The rest of the afternoon passed. Once Pauline brought her a little sheaf of telephone messages. One was from Jim, dated two days before, and Pauline told her, with a slanting look, that she had given the commander the phone number of Belle's apartment. The other messages were from acquaintances and friends of Marcus', and Pauline had referred them to Mr. Woodard or Mr. Gould. She added, "And this man, this window washer. He phoned once or twice. I knew his voice when he came to the kitchen door. That is why I thought perhaps Madame should see him."

Again it struck Sue that there was something different about Pauline, something a little furtive and secretive.

She had dinner downstairs. With the feeling that she was standing only on her own feet now and that she must establish a pattern of her own, she had it served properly at the long dining-room table. Pauline, who had an innate sense of the proprieties, seemed to approve. The reflections of lighted candles wavered dimly in the polished mahogany, and she had used the lace table mats and one of the best dessert plates.

Sue took her coffee upstairs and turned on the terrace lights. The evening had grown still and a little sultry, as if rain might be brewing. One of the porters had brought up a few terrace chairs from the basement storeroom. She sat down on one of them and looked out over the lights glimmering from the towers across the park and in tiers from the buildings around her. She wondered which roof the little man had been standing on. She hadn't asked him that, nor his name either.

The awning supports still stood bare in the pale light. She'd been intending to look up the name of the awning storage house before everything had happened. She thought vaguely again about Rose's day book; she ought to find the address. Now that the weather had turned warmer, the hot sun would beat down upon the terrace and in through the long windows of the gallery and the living room. The pale yellows and soft greens of silk and damask which Rose had selected should not be exposed to the hot glare of the sun. Suddenly it seemed remarkable to be thinking about such unimportant details.

She debated telephoning to Jim, but she wasn't sure whether he was still at Bethesda Naval Hospital. Besides, at that hour of the night it was unlikely that anybody would call him to the telephone. And long-distance numbers could be traced.

There was a flash of lightning to the west. A jet plane streaked like a lovely arrow across the night sky, and she envied the people sitting at ease in that long, lighted cabin, leaving everything behind them, going swiftly to something new and faraway. She could never live in the penthouse now that it was haunted.

She sat up at that. But it *was* haunted. The shadow seemed to have returned to the corner. The hedge where Marcus had fallen was dim in the pale lights, but she seemed to be able to see the broken branches.

Aubrey must see to it that whatever the arrangements about Marcus' estate, she need not live on here. Actually, she wanted nothing that had belonged to Marcus. Besides, in the future . . . Her thoughts leaped ahead. Why, in the future she would go with Jim wherever he went.

But as Belle had told her, she mustn't let herself dream about the future now. She forced her winging thoughts back to the present. She would stay in the apartment only long enough to store the furniture and clear up the endless details. Suddenly she didn't like the lonely stillness of the terrace. She took her coffee cup, went into the house and closed and bolted its door.

For a moment she thought of asking Pauline to come up to the second floor and sleep on the sofa or in Marcus' room that night. But that wouldn't do; there was nothing to hurt her, nothing to haunt her. She made her little tour of the whole house, though, testing each door. Pauline had been ahead of her; everything was locked up tight.

She came back upstairs and examined all the windows to make sure that none was open far enough to permit—well, to permit anyone to enter the house. Nerves, she told herself, and heartily wished that she had gone back to Belle's apartment for the night. But this was silly; she couldn't permit herself to be incapacitated by fancies and fears. In her bedroom she thought of the box with Jim's letters and her ring. Though Conti had disclaimed knowing anything about it, she didn't quite believe him; if he was telling the truth, then who could have taken it? Who would want it?

There was no reasonable answer to either question. Suddenly she asked herself who could have got into the apartment during her absence? Pauline, of course, and Duffy, the superintendent. Aside from her own set, there were no other keys—she caught herself; what about Marcus'? His key ring must have been in a pocket when they found him. But probably these had been given to Aubrey, who would eventually return them to her. The disappearance of the candy box was more important, and the window washer was not only important but dangerous.

Soon Conti, knowing not only that Jim had come to the house in Marcus' company, but also of his return later, would question Jim. And Jim would then tell the lieutenant everything he knew, and she couldn't prevent it. Obviously, if Marcus had been murdered, the question of who might have done it was obscured for her not only by the facts she knew, but by her lack of knowledge of Marcus' life. She knew only one side of his life, just as she had known slightly one side of Rose's. There was a huge chapter of their life together which was obscure to her—their friends and perhaps their enemies in his native city. Marcus could have been murdered by someone she had never met or even heard of, and for a reason which went far back, even before Rose's murder.

From the living room, high-pitched and musical, came the chimes of the French clock, striking twelve times. She turned off the lamp beside her bed, but left a light burning across the room upon the small table beside the chaise longue where Belle had rested on the night following Marcus' death. She was sure that she couldn't sleep, but she had almost dozed off when the telephone rang. It was Jim.

She came awake at once. "Where are you?"

"Back in New York."

"Has Conti talked to you?"

"No. Why?"

"I've got to see you."

"I'll come now."

"Oh, no! No. Tomorrow. Say, at the same bench, about three?"

"All right, but—all right. Is anybody with you?"

"Pauline. I'm not afraid."

Jim said, "You'd better go back to Belle's tomorrow."

She had an uneasy feeling that someone might be listening to their conversation; yet somehow she doubted that the police would do this. "What did the doctors at Bethesda say?"

"Oh, that. I'm okay. Nothing wrong but the malaria. I have to keep quinine on hand, that's all."

"How about the concussion?"

"Okay. They turned me inside out, everything. Told me I was very tough. Try to sleep. Tomorrow at three. If you're held up by anything"— she thought, He means the police— "I'll wait." Then he said good night and hung up.

His voice represented the normal world. She would see him even if an army of plainclothesmen trailed her. He was alive and he had returned, and she knew now that she would be able to sleep.

She awoke suddenly with a sense of some sound in the room. But she could hear only the dull murmur of distant, lonely traffic in the night, the low roar of ventilators, the muffled throb of the pulse of the city which never quite stops and sleeps. There were no footsteps, no rustle of movement, no nearby sounds at all. Then she realized that the room was a black void. She had left a light burning. She turned on the beside lamp quickly before her fancies could terrify her. Nobody was in the room; everything was exactly as she had left it except that the lamp beside the chaise longue was no longer lit. Perhaps the bulb had burned out.

Quickly again, as though, if she waited, something would come out of the night, she scrambled out of bed, ran across the room and turned on the switch of the lamp beside the chaise longue. It glowed out at once. She was sure that she had gone to sleep with the light still burning; yet it did not seem likely that anybody could have broken into the apartment, entered her room without her knowledge and turned off the light.

The suitcase she had brought back from Belle's stood on a luggage rack, its catches open. Undoubtedly Pauline had unpacked it when she turned down the bed. But when Sue lifted the lid, she saw that it had not been unpacked. Its contents were jumbled up as if somebody had searched through it blindly in the dark. She stared down at the melée of dresses, the lingerie and toilet articles. She had packed everything very neatly, and it contained nothing which could be of the slightest interest to anybody.

The click of the catches might have awakened her. She should call the police. That was sensible.

It was anything but sensible. The suitcase was packed so lightly that the objects in it might have jumbled themselves together when she carried it. There was nobody in the apartment but herself and Pauline. Nobody could get in. There was no prowler, nobody who could conceivably be interested in her suitcase. She listened, and heard only the deep murmur of the city.

After a while she went back to bed; after a while she found a book on the bedside table, and she sat holding it, pretending to read, until dawn streaked across the terrace. Then she went to sleep, waking groggily only when Pauline brought her a breakfast tray and told her that it was nearly noon. She also brought an envelope from Aubrey, delivered by a messenger from his office. The envelope contained the small and tragic contents of Marcus' pockets. She returned everything but the keys to the envelope; as Pauline watched, she put the key ring in her handbag. There was also a note from Aubrey, saying that Senator Stidger wished to ask a great favor of her and that he would bring him to call, if convenient, later that day.

In the morning light the room was so ordinary that it denied the presence of anything at all which might walk in the darkness and open and search a suitcase.

Pauline coughed and hovered.

Sue said, "Yes, what is it, Pauline?"

"I was only thinking of the slip covers, madame. I sent them to be cleaned and stored last fall. Should they be sent for now? The sun is growing very bright in the afternoon."

No matter what happened, housekeeping went on. Meals were cooked and eaten; rooms were cleaned and aired; slip covers were put on chairs and sofas to protect delicate colors from the glare of the sun.

Pauline pulled her white apron around back to front and retied the bow. "The phone number might be in Mrs. Desart's book—I mean the first Mrs. Desart."

"It must be in the living room. I had it the day—the day of the accident." She remembered how Aubrey had jumped up, all but lost his balance and knocked Rose's day book to the floor. Belle had picked it up later and then had talked about Rose.

Pauline satisfied herself as to the white bow on her stomach and slid her apron into a more usual position. "Has Madame looked at the book? I mean, the menus and the recipes?"

"Have I—no, not really, Pauline, I've only glanced at it."

"Ah. Beautiful recipes," Pauline said and whisked out of the room. Again it struck Sue that there was that difference in Pauline, something at once bold and at the same time oddly furtive. But of course she knew as well as anyone else that the police were investigating Marcus' death as if they knew it to be murder. She wondered momentarily what Pauline's opinion was and then felt sure that she too believed that it had been murder.

At a quarter to three she went to meet Jim. Again it was a sparkling clear April day. Jim had not arrived, so she sat down at the bench to wait. Presently she looked at her watch; she walked a block north, returned, walked south a block, returned. A man on a bench not far away caught her attention; something about him was familiar. He was not looking at her; indeed he was carefully turned from her as if to hide his face. His bare head showed red hair, streaked lightly with gray; he had broad shoulders and the deadly patient look of a cat at a mousehole; he was Lieutenant Conti.

She was thankful that Jim had not arrived. She must try to get the lieutenant away from here before Jim came. She had to have time to persuade Jim before he talked to Conti that he should omit at least some of the uglier details of his talk with Marcus.

She rose, walked boldly up to Conti and said, "Good afternoon."

He turned and rose. She said, "Why are you following me?"

"I'm not following you," he replied pleasantly. "I'm waiting to see Commander Locke. Oh"—his green eyes narrowed—"here he is." But his face looked so puzzled that Sue whirled around. A taxi had pulled in to the curb and a procession of figures was emerging from it.

Aubrey came first, tidily tugging at his coat. Then Jim jumped out and turned to pay the taxi driver. Senator Stidger came next, bolting out like a rabbit and looking rather like one. Finally, to Sue's disbelief, Pauline stepped out, neat and composed in her blue-and-white-striped uniform.

The four marched toward them across the sidewalk. Pauline was the first to speak. "Madame, it was the window washer. I couldn't help it. He came back."

chapter 15

Jim came and stood beside Sue. As she glanced at him the park seemed to change and the sky became a different color; for she knew that the story of the window washer was going to come out and pour itself into Lieutenant Conti's ears and she knew that Jim had decided to tell everything he knew.

Somehow Jim quieted down Pauline, who was skittering about between French and English. He interrupted Aubrey, who kept saying, "Leave this to me. I'll explain. Leave this to me—" Senator Stidger didn't need any encouragement to remain silent; he eyed a passing bus with obvious and passionate longing to escape.

Jim spoke calmly and with authority. "The window washer is at Mrs. Desart's apartment. He's drunk. Nobody can do anything with him."

Pauline broke in, speaking to Sue, "Madame, I could not call the superintendent to get rid of him or the police or anyone. I could not because he said—" She gulped and gave Lieutenant Conti a look, and Jim said coolly, "He says he saw me push Marcus over the wall. He didn't tell me because I didn't see him. But Pauline and the Senator and Gould all heard him—"

Lieutenant Conti broke in, "Wait a minute. What's this all about?"

Everybody except Senator Stidger started to explain again. But Jim's was the only voice Sue heard and she wished she couldn't. "It seems that a window washer came to Sue—Mrs. Desart—and asked for money. He said that he had been on the roof of another building and that he had seen me plant the terrace flowers, talk to Marcus Desart and then push him over the wall. He wanted money to keep quiet. Now they tell me he's back at her apartment, drunk and noisy—"

"I think we'd better see him," said Lieutenant Conti and waved down a taxi.

This time they got into two taxis. Sue sat between Pauline and Senator Stidger in the first one, Pauline babbling and the Senator shrunk into the corner and clearly wishing himself elsewhere.

"You understand, madame," Pauline babbled. "He threatened. He was drunk. He said terrible things. I could not call the superintendent or anybody else to hear these terrible accusations. I could not call the police for the same reason—"

Senator Stidger said suddenly but remotely, "But you did tell the police. You told this lieutenant."

"But I didn't know that he would be there," Pauline cried.

"It doesn't matter," Sue said desperately. "He was sure to hear of it one way or another." Jim had made up his mind to take action, she thought, and there was nothing to be done.

"And then you see," Pauline babbled feverishly on, "just then the Senator and Mr. Gould came. They couldn't do anything with him either."

Senator Stidger broke in coldly. "The man was drunk and violent. It would have made a scene to throw him out. He would have put up a fight—he's drunk enough for that. Aubrey thought that the quickest way to shut him up and get rid of him was to find you. The man insisted upon seeing you. He shouted—" The Senator winced. "Really unpleasant. Your domestic—Pauline—said that she thought that you had gone to meet Commander Locke."

"Madame, I happened to overhear your conversation last night making the appointment. I merely happened to take up the receiver when the phone rang, and so I knew that you were to meet him at the park. I didn't know which park bench, but then the commander arrived in the lobby as we departed, and he knew where you were to meet him, so we came all together and—that man, that window washer is still in the penthouse," she finished gloomily.

"Very unpleasant," the Senator said.

Pauline muttered to herself. "Broken glass. Broken windows. Anything can happen. He insisted he wouldn't leave until he saw Madame. So"—here Pauline sighed and produced that fine French shrug which disclaims responsibility for anything and everything—"so we came for Madame."

It was all perfectly logical in a confusing and frightening way. Nobody can ever control events, Sue thought dismally; nobody can ever guess in advance what anybody else will do. She couldn't even blame Pauline as she would have liked to do; she would have liked to blame anybody, just then.

The second taxi drew up at the apartment house thirty seconds behind them. Polk was not yet on duty, and the other doorman was not in sight. As they marched through the lobby, their footsteps sounding ominous, the new elevator man stood watching them. He was a young fellow, spruce in the dark blue and brass-buttoned uniform of the apartment house employees, and he looked acutely curious.

As they got into the cage, the lieutenant said mildly, "Now then, Orry, is this the man you took up to the eleventh floor on the afternoon Mr. Desart . . . died?" He indicated Jim.

The boy gave Jim a glance, gulped and said, "Yes, sir."

"How about the delivery man, the man with the box? Could he have been Commander Locke?"

"I don't know, sir. I couldn't see his face." With obvious relief the boy stopped the elevator at the eleventh floor and the door slid back.

"Thank you, son," Conti said. Jim said nothing.

When Sue unlocked the door, there was no sound in the penthouse. She had expected loud noises, singing, shouting, the crash of glass as Pauline had gloomily suggested—anything at all but silence. Jim sprang up the stairs ahead of Lieutenant Conti, and she followed.

The window washer was gone. A thorough search produced no signs even of his ever having been there.

Conti went straight to the point. "Mrs. Desart, as you know, your maid, Mr. Gould and the Senator all heard the window washer say that he saw the commander kill Mr. Desart. But what exactly did he say to you?"

They all knew; but she told it reluctantly nevertheless.

"He was trying to blackmail me. He said that he saw a man in a blue uniform—he said it was Jim—on the terrace. He said that he saw Marcus fall. But he must have invented it. He kept talking about a reward. He meant blackmail."

"Is that all he said? I mean, were there any details? Tell me word for word slowly."

She told Conti everything that she could remember. When she repeated the window washer's claim about seeing the man in the uniform planting the flowers, she thought there was a brighter flicker in the lieutenant's eyes. But when she finished he said only, "May I use the phone?"

Pauline led him to the telephone in Sue's bedroom. Senator Stidger sat down and shut his eyes. Aubrey wandered to a window and looked out. Sue said, "Jim, where were you? Why didn't you meet me? What happened?"

"It's all right," Jim said quietly. "While we were in the taxi I told Conti about Marcus' refusing a divorce. He knew that I had returned here a second time that afternoon."

At the telephone in the bedroom they heard Conti saying, "—and I want him found. Here's his description—" Apparently he turned to Pauline, who obliged with a swift and remarkably accurate description. When her excited voice stopped, Conti took over again. "Call every window-cleaning establishment—"

Senator Stidger opened his eyes and looked at Aubrey. "I don't think we should talk to Mrs. Desart just now, Aubrey. I have to get the plane back to Washington."

Aubrey said, "I expect you're right. You see, Sue, we—that is, the Senator intended to ask you to—that is, as you know, Marcus was very popular in his home, very well liked. We thought—perhaps I suggested it—that if you and Belle would appear with him at various political meetings during his campaign at home, dinners and all that—I mean, merely lend him your support—that is, Marcus' decision to run and then his sudden death might have a bad effect, split the party so that they might want to select another candidate. Anything can happen, you know, and the Senator believed that your public support—"

"You believe it, Aubrey," the Senator said in a steely voice. "I myself think anything of the sort is quite unnecessary. Besides, the commander's return and everything else is bound to get in the newspapers soon. I'm sorry, Mrs. Desart, but frankly I don't want your support any more. Now I really must leave." He bowed to Sue and left.

Aubrey said dolefully, "He means that your support might do more harm than good. He may be right. Not that it matters to me, except—well, if I can do a favor for anybody, naturally—"

"Especially if he's in a position of power," Jim said softly.

Aubrey flushed bright pink. "Really, Locke, it was not necessary to tell Conti everything! A quarrel with Marcus! His refusal to consider a divorce! Your two visits here the very afternoon he died! How could you be such a fool! How could you put poor Sue in such a terrible position!"

"Jim," Sue said. "You didn't answer me. Why didn't you meet me at the park? Why did you come here instead?" It didn't matter, and she wondered vaguely why she was asking.

"I didn't meet you at the park because Conti came to the club to see me, and I had decided that we must tell him everything we knew. But I wanted to talk to you before I did, so when they told me he was waiting for me, I got away by a service elevator and came here. I expect the man who followed us that day, the man with the red tie, told Conti where we had met. He took the chance of finding us at the same place, and that's why he was there with you when we all drove up."

Lieutenant Conti returned, Pauline hovering behind him. "They'll find the window washer. Of course, you should have told me about him at once, Mrs. Desart. Where's the Senator?"

Aubrey said, "He had to go back to Washington. Lieutenant Conti, the Senator really had nothing to do with Marcus' death. Are you saying that Marcus was murdered?"

Lieutenant Conti sat down and crossed his long legs. "I'm not holding anybody for questioning—at least not yet."

"That's no answer." Aubrey was scarlet. "Locke, you do know that you have a right to legal counsel, don't you? You needn't answer any questions at all without legal counsel. If you want me to act for you, I'll do so. I refuse to believe that Marcus was murdered. If all this gets into the newspapers, neither you nor Sue will ever be able to live it down. I don't like it, I—"

"All right, Counselor," Conti said mildly. "I'm going to ask the commander a question or two. If he doesn't want to answer, he doesn't have to."

"But he's already told you everything," Aubrey burst out. "On the way over here in the cab. I never heard anybody talk so fast and say so much!"

Conti smiled. Aubrey shouted, "It's a serious business! Nothing funny or—now, Locke, don't say any more. *Just keep quiet.*"

"What do you want to ask me, Conti?" Jim said. "You have it all in a nutshell, really. I came here the night before Marcus died and saw Sue—Mrs. Desart. I came here in the morning to tell Mrs. Desart that I intended to go to see Marcus and tell him of my return. I couldn't find him at his office, so I came back that afternoon and met him in the lobby. He brought me up here not knowing who I was. Then we talked, and he refused to give Sue a divorce. We did, however, agree to talk to each other again—that is, it was implicit—and I went away. But about an hour or so later—I can't be sure of the time—I came back because I felt that nothing had really been settled. There you have it."

"In the meantime your husband struck you, isn't that right, Mrs. Desart?"

So at least Jim had not told him that, Sue thought. Aubrey cried, "Don't answer, Sue! You're not obliged to answer."

But Lieutenant Conti wouldn't believe her denial; he had seen the bruises on her face. She nodded, still humiliated and ashamed at the memory. Jim said, "She went out then. She walked for a long time. When she came back—"

"All right, Commander," Conti said. "I'll talk to Mrs. Desart myself. Now then, the second time you returned here that afternoon might have been just before or just after Mr. Desart fell. What is your idea about that?"

It did not sound like a trap, but like a perfectly sensible inquiry. Jim said, "I don't know. I don't know when he fell. I'm not sure what time it was when I came the second time and rang the doorbell. I do know that I wasn't here long enough to be let into the apartment and to get Mr. Desart out on the terrace and kill him—much less to plant the flowers. The window washer says that the man in uniform he saw—if in fact he saw anybody—planted all those little flowers. I wouldn't have had time for that."

"That's a point!" Aubrey cried. "That's a point, Lieutenant."

Conti seemed to think this over, and then said mildly, "Of course, this window washer could have learned of

Locke's return and his former engagement to Mrs. Desart in a number of ways."

"Everybody knew it!" Sue said. "Everybody in the apartment house—"

"Very likely." Conti turned to Aubrey. "Were Mr. Desart and the Senator on good terms?"

"Why, yes, certainly. That is, of course, the Senator quite rightly opposed Marcus' decision to re-enter politics. I agreed with the Senator."

Jim said, "What's Senator Stidger's public record?"

Aubrey shouted. "Splendid! Nothing that Marcus—" he caught himself.

Sue said, "Marcus said that the Senator had obliged him to say things in the privacy of his own home that he'd rather not say publicly. What things, Aubrey?"

Aubrey nearly wrung his hands. "Marcus was only talking. Trying to scare the Senator. Marcus—well, he had certain tactics. I swear to you"—he turned to Conti—"that Senator Stidger's record is perfectly clear. Ask anybody. His family life, his business affairs—why, he got rid of every single investment that could possibly cause a conflict of interest in his public life. Of course," he added condescendingly, "he's not the dramatic figure that Marcus was. He's not the orator, hasn't got the gift, the flair, the magnetism, the vote-getting ability, whatever it is that sways people. But he's a good man and an honest one, and I was shocked—shocked, I tell you, when Marcus attacked him."

"And your own interest?" Conti said, mildly again. "Your own feelings about Mr. Desart re-entering public life?"

"I was against it, naturally. The firm had suffered during the investigation following Rose's—his wife's—murder. It was a well-known case. Good heavens, everybody was talking about it. The firm suffered. There are still clients who don't want *him.* The trouble was, of course, that you—the police, that is—never were able to find the murderer, and . . . No," Aubrey said flatly. "I wasn't going to go through all that again. And I knew that the minute it was so much as rumored that Marcus intended to seek election, the whole ugly story would be dredged up. I didn't want that, so I phoned Stidger to come here and try to stop Marcus."

Conti said thoughtfully, "I get the impression that you and Senator Stidger are quite close friends."

Aubrey pulled out another beautiful handkerchief. "Friends? He's never been a client of ours, if that's what you want to know."

"You let him know immediately that Mr. Desart had decided to run for office. That same night."

"Yes, because I thought he would be able to talk Marcus out of it."

"Were you at this political dinner?"

"No. Oh, I see. You want to know who told me of Marcus' decision. There's always somebody who tells you these things; in this case it was Sam Dodson. He's an old friend of Marcus', from home. He knows me slightly, and he was in doubt about the wisdom of backing Marcus. Sam phoned me as soon as he left the dinner that night to get my opinion. I thought it over, phoned the Senator and he came up on the morning plane. It's as simple as that, Lieutenant."

"Very simple," the lieutenant said. He looked at Jim. "Why did you go to the public library this morning?"

"Oh," Jim said. "So you were there too."

"It occurred to me that some people might wish to refresh their memories about Rose Desart's murder. I discovered that I was the third person to ask recently for those particular newspaper files. I must have missed you by moments early this morning. Did you know that Marcus Desart spent part of the last morning of his life in the public library, looking at those same files?"

A small detail flashed across Sue's memory: the rim of dust on Marcus' usually immaculate cuff, the kind of dust that accumulates in spite of everything in a big city. So he had been thinking of Rose, thinking of running for office again, wondering whether the accounts of Rose's murder might affect his campaign.

Conti, watching her, said quietly, "It is possible, I suppose, that your husband found some clue to his wife's murder which up until then had not struck him as evidence."

Aubrey said, "No! It's not possible! Marcus would have—have told me!"

After a moment Conti said, "Such a piece of evidence—or rather the discovery of such a piece of evidence on Mr. Desart's part—would certainly provide motivation for his murder by a person who might be endangered by that evidence."

Jim said, "You mean if Marcus got the goods on somebody and told him about it, then that somebody killed Marcus."

Conti said, "That could have happened, I suppose. But I went through every word of the newspaper stories about the murder, as well as the police file, and I've found nothing new." He glanced at his watch. "I should have heard something about this window washer before now. Commander, have you any objection to my seeing your fitness and medical reports?"

Jim suddenly grinned, honestly amused. "Go ahead, Lieutenant, you'd see them anyway without my permission. But you'll find that there are no effects of concussion and that my malaria is under control. So no matter what happens, I'm not likely to plead war wounds, temporary blackout, delirium or anything—"

"Good heavens," Aubrey cried, shocked. "I'm thankful there's no record of this admission. A dangerous admission, Locke. If I were defending you—"

"I haven't been accused by the police of anything yet," Jim said pleasantly.

Ignoring Aubrey, Conti said, "I expect the window washer left by the service elevator. I'll talk to the operator. Mrs. Desart, this private elevator of yours—Duffy tells me that he can operate the main switch but that he has no key for the elevator itself."

"I don't know. I never thought of that."

"How many keys are there and who has them?" Conti asked.

"Why, I have one. My husband had one—which I have now. Pauline has one. That's all."

Conti eyed the polished toe of one oxford. "M'm," he said finally. "I see. You're sure that there are no other keys?"

Sue hesitated. "I think I'd know it if anyone else had a key."

Conti lifted green eyes to Pauline. "Do you agree with Mrs. Desart?"

Pauline looked taken aback; her thin eyelids fluttered. "Why, I—why, yes, Lieutenant. Yes, certainly. I mean no, certainly. No other keys."

"M'm," Conti said again, looked at his other oxford, rose, said, "Thank you all very much," and walked across the gallery and down the stairs.

As Pauline started after him, Sue said, "Wait, Pauline. Are you sure there are no other keys? You see, if somebody could get into the apartment—"

"Oh, I'm sure, madame. I'm sure," Pauline said glibly, and scurried off after Lieutenant Conti. The hall door downstairs banged smartly.

Aubrey gave himself a kind of shake, looked at Sue and at Jim, shook his head, opened his mouth, shut it again and made a kind of wave with one manicured hand before he too marched, head up, erect and spruce, across the gallery and down the stairs.

Jim said quietly, "I had to tell Conti everything, Sue. I meant to talk to you first, though."

"I don't suppose it matters. He already knew that you'd been here and all about your being reported dead and then coming back. He asked me about it. But he didn't know that you and Marcus had such a dreadful quarrel, and—"

"Well, he doesn't really know that now," Jim said equably, "although he certainly guesses it. He admits that he went to the library to see whether anybody else had been looking at the same files. It might have given him some kind of lead."

"Was there anything at all, Jim?"

"Not that I could see. But I can't help thinking that there just might be something which at the time meant nothing to Marcus, but all at once did have significance the day he died. Do you think he'd have done nothing about it? I don't. From what I saw of Marcus, he'd raise hell immediately. He'd try to nail down the evidence, prove it to himself though, before he went to the police. It's just possible that this happened. It's also possible," he added flatly, "that nothing at all happened."

"Jim, he'd have told me. No, he probably *wouldn't* have told me. Besides, he had no chance to. But now you've put yourself in Conti's hands. Don't you see how dangerous—?"

Jim came over and took her hands. "Sue, I tell you, we

cannot go through life with the question of Marcus' death hanging over our heads. It's got to be settled one way or another. We have to take the risk. We can't let any questions remain unanswered. We have our whole life to live together."

"It's not going to be easy."

"It's worth it. Besides," he added dryly, "Conti already knew most of what I told him. Now then, when I phoned you last night you had something on your mind. You sounded scared. Why?"

She was tired and bewildered and felt as if she'd been through a whirlwind. "The window washer. I was going to tell you about him. You phoned before somebody . . . But that was only a nightmare, nothing at all—"

Jim's face changed. "*What* was only a nightmare?"

"Oh, I thought somebody was in my room in the middle of the night. But there wasn't anybody. The light had been turned off. I thought I'd left it turned on, but really nobody could have been here."

"Tell me about it."

There was nothing to tell, but she gave him her nebulous and unconvincing details. "I must have been dreaming. Oh, yes, and they took the candy box while I was staying with Belle. I haven't had a chance to tell you about that. The police took it—only Conti says they didn't."

"What candy box?"

She told him, and when she had finished he leaned over and kissed her as tenderly as if murder and violence and suspicion had never existed. But then before she could lean her head against him as she wanted to do, he moved away, "Perhaps you made a mistake, Sue. It doesn't matter really, because Conti knows all about us, but go and look for the box. Perhaps you were mistaken."

"No, I wasn't mistaken. I'll look, but—" She ran into her bedroom, opened the lower drawer and groped beneath the lingerie. Immediately her fingers encountered the worn corners of the candy box.

chapter 16

Sue drew the box out and took it in to Jim.

When he opened it his face softened. "I'll get you a bigger diamond sometime, Sue. What's that?"

"That" was the battered folder which had once held matches. "We had dinner at that restaurant on the day I first knew that I loved you. Silly—"

He didn't look at her as he closed the box deliberately; placing it on the table, he said softly, "I wasn't going to touch you." Then he turned, took her in his arms and put his face against her cheek. After a moment he turned her head a little so their lips could meet, and for a moment everything else in the world was forgotten.

But then Jim removed her arms, which had clasped themselves tight around him. "I didn't mean to. I couldn't help it—oh, I did mean to, of course. I'll always—" He took a long breath. "All right, Sue. All right, my darling."

It made no sense, but she understood him. "Jim, if they charge you with murder, how can we prove you didn't kill him?"

"The police aren't fools."

"They want Rose's murderer! They want to prove that Marcus was murdered—"

"Wait, now, Sue. Certainly they'd like to close the case of Rose's murder, but they want real evidence, nothing else."

"They took this box! Conti lied to me!"

"Are you sure?"

"I'm not being hysterical! I *know* that box was gone. Now it's back, so it must have been the police."

"But suppose it wasn't the police. Perhaps it was somebody who can come and go in this apartment without being seen. You said there were only three keys to the private elevator?"

"Yes. Pauline's, mine and Marcus'. That's all. No, wait—Aubrey had Marcus' keys. He sent them back to me, but I suppose there was time to have another key made."

Jim considered this. "I can't imagine Aubrey tiptoeing around here at night; he's simply too elegant. Searching a suitcase? Creeping around a dark apartment? Mmn. Still, what do you know about him, Sue? Has he a family?"

"No. That is, his wife died—oh, years ago. I didn't know her. He's very popular, invited everywhere. Hostesses love him."

"Good for Aubrey." Jim grinned a little. "I know that he didn't want Marcus to run for office, but did he have any other quarrel with him?"

"No. I think I'd have known, or at least guessed. Of course, he does profit by Marcus' death! You haven't heard about Marcus' will." She told him quickly about it, including the reason for Belle's refusal to take the money.

Jim was suprised. "Do you think she really believes that Marcus killed Rose?"

"Oh, I don't know. If he did, though, then who would kill Marcus—that is, if his death *is* connected with Rose's murder?"

"Why, Belle Minot, of course," Jim said.

"Belle! No!"

"If she thought that he killed her daughter, she certainly had a motive."

"Not Belle! And after six years!"

"There has to be some motive—that is, if it was murder. It came so immediately after Marcus' decision to run for office that this also could be a motive. I suppose the police are considering it; it's obvious. Yet who would want to stop him except Senator Stidger or Aubrey Gould?"

"I would have stopped him if I could," Sue said in a low voice. "I had encouraged him before I knew you were alive. Then I wished I hadn't."

"You did what you thought was best," Jim said matter-of-factly. "Now, another motive might be money. Belle gets his money."

"She wouldn't take it. I told you!"

"Sue, you believe that Marcus was murdered and so do I. I'm sure that Aubrey thinks so too, though he denies it. There's no doubt about Conti; all he wants is some firm evidence of murder. He's too smart to stick his neck out without evidence. He'll get it from the window washer."

"Against you."

"Maybe not. Now, if somebody got into this apartment last night, he had a reason, and if he broke into the place while you were staying at Belle's, he was looking for something. The only thing that disappeared was this candy box, and now it's back. Perhaps it was returned last night."

"It really *was* gone, Jim."

"Okay, why? There's nothing secret in it. Our engagement was announced. No, I think that whoever took it didn't open it at once. I suspect that he snatched it and took it away; maybe somebody was coming—he was in a hurry."

"I still think it was the police. The house had been searched—that is, the living room and my bedroom."

"Didn't Pauline know it?"

"She says not, and I believe her. But of course she wasn't in the house all the time. Jim, Belle *couldn't* have pushed Marcus over that wall. For one thing, it's physically impossible. She's so small and—"

"And very charming. She could have coaxed Marcus up on that wall to tie up the willow, couldn't she?"

"She *wouldn't*."

Jim went through the gallery onto the terrace, and Sue followed. It was late afternoon and the sun was casting soft shades of mauve, rose-red and pale gold over the towers around them. The sky was a deep blue, with a few white clouds that seemed very near. The colors were as clear as if a fine artist had chosen them from his palette.

Jim said thoughtfully, "This man in a blue uniform that Orry saw. Conti asked me about him in the taxi. I wasn't carrying any box!"

"Orry didn't identify you positively."

"That's something," Jim said. "Of course, half the delivery men and doormen in town wear blue uniforms. Oh, well, we can't get anywhere until Conti finds this window washer and learns how much he really saw and how much he invented. If there really was a man in blue on the terrace, talking to Marcus and then pushing him over the edge, the window washer ought to be able to identify him. But the only thing that makes me credit his story is his claim that this man was planting the flowers. Somehow I don't think he'd have made that up."

"N-no. Unless Marcus was planting them."

"Do you really think that Marcus tied up that tree?"

"He might have been ashamed of striking me; maybe he was trying to please me by finishing the flowers."

"I know so little about Marcus. What about Woody? He inherited a handsome sum. Maybe he needs it."

"Woody and Marcus were very close, and besides, Woody has a good practice. He wanted Marcus to run for office, and there was an idea—that is, it came from Belle, really—that if Marcus was elected, Woody might go to Washington with him in some capacity. I think Woody wanted that. He—" She paused for a second, thinking. "It never occurred to me before now, but I think that Woody is ambitious—politically ambitious. Otherwise he wouldn't have taken such a direct interest in getting Marcus to run for office."

"So Marcus was valuable to him? But Marcus might be more certainly valuable dead. Fifty thousand dollars."

"I don't think he knew that—in fact, I'm sure he didn't. He seemed really moved by the news. Besides, Woody had saved Marcus' life only the day before. Marcus had been up on the wall, trying to tie up that tree; he was dizzy, and Woody ran out and caught him just in time. If he'd wanted Marcus to die, all he had to do was let him go then."

"Tell me how it happened."

She told Jim slowly, even remembering the floating piece

of green twine that had warned her. "Lieutenant Conti questioned me about it the next morning."

"What did he ask you?"

"How it happened—all that. Whether anyone else had been here besides me and Woody and Pauline. Nobody was. But then Conti went over and looked through the gate, and it struck me at the time that maybe he thought someone had seen the whole thing from there."

Jim walked over to the wrought-iron gate. "It would be easy enough. I suppose Conti thought that someone might have been watching and that what had happened suggested a neat way of murder."

Sue thought back to that drizzly spring day. "I think I'd have seen anyone. But no, perhaps not. When I saw Marcus wavering on the parapet and Woody running to catch him, I wouldn't have noticed anything else."

Jim walked back slowly, his hands in his pockets, frowning. "I'm not sure that saving a man's life one day proves that you are not capable of killing him the next. Still, it has a certain weight." He sighed. "I hope they've found the window washer by now."

From the door to the gallery, Pauline announced, "Madame, there's a lady." She proffered a slip of paper on the little silver tray to Sue.

"Miss Jean Wilson," Sue read, puzzled for a moment.

Pauline's black eyes were bright. "She was once Mr. Desart's secretary."

"Oh, of course. Ask her to come upstairs, Pauline."

While they waited she said to Jim, "I don't know her. She was his secretary long ago, before he moved to New York. She's in Marcus' will."

"How much?"

"A thousand dollars."

Jim shook his head. "Not enough for a murder motive. Oh, Sue, get that look off your face. We'll come out of this all right. Do you want me to leave?"

"It doesn't matter now," she said flatly. "Everybody knows about you."

"Miss Wilson," Pauline said very properly from the doorway.

Whatever Sue might have expected, Jean Wilson was not it. She came out on the terrace gracefully, soberly, eying them both. A strapping big woman, her thick golden hair was closely cut and showed the fine lines of a beautiful head; she had deep-set hazel eyes, an intelligent forehead and full lips. She also had a sense of style which was obvious at once; she wore a dark gray suit elegant in its simplicity, a handsome emerald and diamond pin and carried a smart handbag. In a low voice she said, "Mrs. Desart?"

Sue put out her hand. Jean Wilson took it and nodded as Sue introduced Jim. Curiously, the aura of her forceful character was as pervasive as perfume. Here, Sue felt, was a woman to be reckoned with—and here, she realized suddenly, was a woman in grief. It was so strong an impression that she had an impulse to reach out to her, to say something friendly and sympathetic. But Jean Wilson forestalled her by saying firmly, "A pleasant view from here. I've always liked it," and striding out to look at the sky and sun-lighted towers.

Pauline still stood in the doorway, and Sue said, "You're just in time for something to drink, Miss Wilson."

The woman's fine hazel eyes turned to meet her own directly. "Thank you. Tea, if it's not too much trouble."

"Bring it out here, please, Pauline," Sue said.

Jean Wilson glanced around, selected a chair and sat down, disposing her long legs and stalwart body with deliberate grace. Her eyelids were swollen and faintly pink; the glare of the setting sun showed sharp lines of fatigue in her face. She glanced at Jim and said, "I know your name, Commander Locke. Marcus told me about you at the time of his new marriage. Also, Aubrey Gould told me that you had returned from the dead, so to speak." Now she looked at Sue and explained, "I saw Aubrey and Woody. I had to know. They told me the—" she swallowed, looked at the parapet and the willow tree and then swiftly away—"the story as you gave it to the police."

Sue saw Jim's face harden. "That's the way it happened," he said.

Jean Wilson took a long breath and linked her large, fine hands. "Mrs. Desart, I think I'm not being immodest when I say that I have a certain tact and diplomacy. I couldn't have held my job without it. But there are times to be direct, and this is one of them. Marcus was murdered."

Jim asked, "Why do you say that, Miss Wilson?"

She lifted one hand. "Because I knew Marcus. But I'm not the only one who thinks so. Why are there policemen at the elevator in the lobby? Why did they ask my name before I was permitted to come up here?"

Sue looked at Jim, who said, "This is news to us. But there's a reason for it. A window washer claims to have seen me kill Marcus."

Jean Wilson's fine eyes were intent. "Why haven't they arrested you?"

"Because they haven't found the window washer and heard his story at first hand. I didn't know until now that there was a police guard, but if I were Lieutenant Conti—that's the man who is in charge of the investigation—I would do exactly that."

Jean Wilson may have been tactful; she could also be as direct as a shotgun. "And did you kill Marcus?"

"No."

Miss Wilson debated this for only an instant. "I came here to tell you that I intended to go to the police and tell them that Marcus was not a man who would commit suicide, and that he certainly was not fool enough to fall off a wall. I intended to tell them that I thought it was murder, but it seemed only fair to tell you my intentions first, Mrs. Desart. Also"—Jean Wilson's eyes had a catlike gleam—"I wanted to see you."

Sue had an uneasy feeling that if she moved a hair Jean would jump. She said, "Marcus was very grateful to you, Miss Wilson. I expect Aubrey Gould told you that he had remembered you in his will."

"Marcus loved me," Jean Wilson said flatly. "And I loved him. He loved me long before he married Rose. He loved me when he married you. He never stopped loving me."

Sue stared at her. After a pause Jim said, "You saw him recently?"

Jean Wilson cast him a contemptuous look. "I have been spending a week in New York. I do that occasionally so I can see Marcus. I may as well tell you that I took a position in Senator Stidger's office in order to be nearer Marcus. Three nights before his death, he told you"—her lambent gaze came back to Sue—"he told you that he was dining with Aubrey, didn't he?"

Sue thought back. "Why yes, there was a night when he went out to dinner. I think he said that it was with Aubrey."

"And we saw each other in the daytime too."

Jim said very gently but firmly, "But he married Sue."

Jean Wilson lifted her hands in a queerly resigned gesture. "He kept saying he didn't know why, except that he felt sorry for her. But I knew why. I haven't a single what Marcus would call "good" connection. What education I've had I've given myself. Marcus was always ambitious. He knew that Rose would grace any position into which he might move. When he married you"—she glanced at Sue coolly— "he did so because he wanted a young wife, somebody he could expect to be a charming hostess. He certainly didn't want anybody saying that he had married a woman he had known so long—so well—even before his first marriage. That marriage caused only a brief separation between us. He came back to me, as I knew he would." Her fine eyes were brilliant, as if there were tears in them, but she spoke without a quaver. "Ambition came first with him—before me, before Rose. He didn't murder Rose, though. He was proud of her beauty and her ability. Besides, he wouldn't have murdered anybody."

Sue looked at the resolute face and at the big, strong hands which were now clasped together, and thought, You knew both Rose and Marcus, and I've never met you before. You could have killed Rose.

Jim said, "When did you last see Marcus, Miss Wilson?"

"The day he was killed. Twice. He came to me early in the morning to tell me of his decision to run for office again. He wanted my help, and my advice too. Then he said that he was going to the public library to look over the accounts of Rose's death again because everything in the newspapers at that time would be dredged up again the moment he announced his candidacy. I offered to go with him, but he wouldn't let me. He never wanted anyone to know about us, you see." When she looked down, her attempt to disguise her swollen eyelids with green eye shadow was pathetically obvious. "That was sensible. I understood it. He always intended to run for office again, you know. He may not have admitted it to anyone, but he was only waiting for the right time. In fact, he had been working for it, but very quietly."

Remembering how she had all but begged him to consider resuming his career, Sue realized she had not known Marcus at all.

After a moment Jim said, "You said that you saw him twice that day?"

"Yes. He had lunch with Woody, Aubrey and Senator Stidger, and then he came to see me directly afterward." So that was why Marcus had not been in his office that afternoon, Sue thought. Jean Wilson went on. "He told me about the lunch. Nothing happened except that Marcus told them his mind was made up. Then he came to tell me and to"—she sighed—"to make me understand that he was counting on my help. He left a little before three."

Jim said, "When you offered to help Marcus, did you . . . May I put it bluntly, Miss Wilson?"

"Please do," said Jean Wilson, with a cutting edge in that clear low voice.

"Did you offer to supply Marcus with ammunition against Senator Stidger?"

She lowered her gleaming hazel eyes again. "He wanted me to. Anything, he said, that he could use against Stidger. Not openly, you understand, but privately to the party leaders at home so that he could get their full support. And yes, I *had* promised that morning to find something against Stidger. But—it doesn't matter now, since Marcus is dead. I know Senator Stidger's affairs because I'm his confidential secretary. The fact is, there is not one thing against Stidger. I don't like him—naturally, I suppose. I was jealous because he was elected instead of Marcus. Nevertheless, I did my job efficiently. I promised Marcus I'd try to find some kind of ammunition against Stidger, but I couldn't think what it would be. Stidger is an able and honest man. I think he was born knowing that sometime he'd be in public office and has behaved accordingly all his life." For the first time Jean Wilson's fine lips curved in a kind of smile. "No, I doubt if I could have trumped up a thing—nothing that would hold water, at any rate."

"You'd have invented something?" Jim said coolly.

She answered in the same tone. "That wouldn't have worked, you know. The main assets we had were Marcus' magnetism, his powers as a speaker, his—his presence. The liking people had for him. I told him he'd win, of course. I wanted him to have what he wanted—even with another wife. But then he was killed." She looked out across the glints of red and gold sunlight on the towers looming against the evening sky, and there was something so deeply musing in her gaze that Sue didn't speak or move. She felt as if Jean Wilson had gone away on a long journey; yet there she sat, still, graceful and beautiful.

After a moment Jim lit a cigarette and walked over to the parapet. He said casually, over his shoulder, "Stidger and Marcus must have known each other for a long time."

Jean Wilson answered absently. "Oh, yes, naturally. Both of them were interested in politics and they were born in the same city. But they were not close friends. I went to work for the Senator after Rose's murder. Up to then I had stayed in Marcus' home office, but his law practice there had begun to diminish when he came East and he and Aubrey became partners. Then when Rose was murdered and he gave up his chance for election, I—oh, I'd had a taste of politics during the beginning of Marcus' campaign, and of course I knew Stidger. I wanted to leave home and—I wanted to be nearer Marcus."

"Did Stidger like Rose?"

Again Jean Wilson replied as if she were thinking of something else. "I think so. Rose was so beautiful—like a bird of paradise. Nobody could help liking her. Even I—sometimes I found myself hating Marcus but admiring Rose. I couldn't really blame her, you see—that is, I couldn't blame her for Marcus' marrying her. But you don't want to hear all this."

"Did Stidger like Rose . . . too much?"

Jean Wilson blinked slowly, focused her brilliant eyes on Jim and laughed. "Stidger! He didn't murder Rose, if that's what you're getting at." She took a long breath and looked intently at Sue; she had indeed been on a long journey of thought. "I've changed my mind," she said evenly. "Perhaps I didn't really intend to tell the police that I thought one of you had murdered Marcus. Perhaps I didn't really intend to tell the police that you had a motive. In any case, since they already know that, it doesn't matter. The real reason I came was because I had to see you. You're not at all what Marcus led me to expect. He had his own rules, you know. I ought to have known that he was lying to me—very adroitly, of course. He said that he felt sorry for you, that you were the daughter of an old friend, that—oh, he made up a convincing story. In the end I really believed that you had managed to catch him and that all you were interested in was his money. You see . . . No, you don't see. I suppose I believed him because I wanted to. I . . . Never mind all this. Usually I'm quick to see through people. You're not what I expected and hated. It's odd," she said, "what a fool an intelligent woman can make of herself. Oh, I understand Marcus. He wanted you for show, but he intended to keep me for everything else."

"He ought to have married you," Sue said, again feeling herself only an observer.

Jean Wilson's fine eyes widened a little; then she smiled and shook her head. "You see me as I am now. Marcus could never forget the big, gawky girl he once employed as a file clerk. In those days I also swept out the office, emptied the ashtrays and sorted the mail. Oh, no, he wouldn't have married me; in fact, I wouldn't have let him. I was ambitious for Marcus too, you see. Rose was a poor wife."

"Rose?" Sue was astonished.

"I had some justification. Rose deserved to be murdered." She rose.

"What do you mean?" Jim said quickly.

Jean Wilson said only, "It's all in the past. I've been here many times, you know, as Rose's husband's employee. I expect she knew the truth, but then she didn't care. She had all she wanted. Too much." She turned toward the door.

Jim said, "Wait, please, Miss Wilson. What do you mean by saying she deserved to be murdered? What had she done?"

"I don't mean anything. Good-bye," said Jean Wilson firmly, and turning to leave, collided with Pauline and a large tray. Cups and teapot crashed, and triangles of honeyed toast skittered over the terrace, gathering soot. In the melee Jean Wilson simply disappeared. Jim disentangled himself from a sputtering Pauline and ran after her.

A tiny lacy napkin fluttered to Sue's feet. She was helping Pauline clear up the debris when Jim returned.

"She's gone. The elevator happened to be right at your floor. No use trying to stop her." He looked at Sue for a long moment. "Well, I'll be damned. In love with Marcus. She didn't like you, naturally, but she hated Rose."

He had forgotten Pauline, who continued to gather up fragments of china. Her black eyes were somber and thoughtful. "My madame knew all about this Miss Wilson," she said. "My madame didn't care. She was admired by everybody." She swept past them both into the penthouse.

chapter 17

Sue took up a silver spoon and stared at it. Finally she said, "But I still don't believe Jean Wilson killed Rose."

Jim walked to the hedge and stood silhouetted against the rosy sky. "She might have. It's a little hard to visualize, but after all, she hated Rose and loved Marcus. She might have killed Rose, but she'd never have killed Marcus."

"No. Marcus must have been a strange man, Jim. I realize now I didn't know him at all."

Jim turned around. "Oh, yes, you knew one side of him—the good side. Don't be too hard on him, Sue. Lots of people have as many colors as a rainbow. He wasn't all good, but he wasn't all bad, either. He was ambitious, I suppose. Jean Wilson helped to explain a number of things."

"I was so sure that he loved only Rose."

"Now we know why Marcus threatened Stidger. He expected Jean to come up with some kind of damaging information, something that would be strong enough to influence his party leaders, or the voters, if necessary. And we also know why Marcus, after refusing firmly to run for office, appeared to change his mind so suddenly. In fact, he had intended to run all along; he only wanted to be urged to do so because it would mean stronger backing for him.

"She said Rose deserved to be murdered."

The city, now strung with bright strings of lights, was tinged in deep violet tones. As always at that hour, the sounds of traffic had quieted to a low murmur. Sue was sitting directly opposite the gap in the wall which provided an entrance to the fire escape. The box of hedge masked the opening, but through the hazy young greens she could glimpse the park, misty and blue now with shadows of coming twilight.

Over his shoulder, Jim said, "Naturally, she didn't like Rose."

"*Everybody* liked Rose. Nobody could have helped liking Rose."

"A woman in love with Marcus could help it. But I understand what you mean; you felt that she had some specific reason for hating Rose. Something that justified her liaison with Marcus. I wonder if the police questioned Jean Wilson after Rose's murder. There was no mention of her name in the newspaper accounts."

Pauline came out with a broom and dustpan and they both moved to help her gather up the debris, but she pushed them aside. "No, no," she said sourly. "The broom will brush it all up."

"Pauline—" Jim hesitated and then plunged ahead. "I

know you were fond of your—of Mrs. Desart. But what did you mean when you said that she knew all about Miss Wilson? Did she tell you?"

"Tell me!" Pauline didn't look up. "It is not necessary to make talk. Women together understand these things."

"But you said that Mrs. Desart didn't care."

"And why should she care? Why should anybody care? Unless," Pauline said, "Miss Wilson came to you for money, madame."

"No, she didn't," Sue said.

Pauline finished brushing bits of china into the dustpan, rose and said, "But of course he gave Miss Wilson jewels. That pin she wore, many other objects of value, I am sure. Advice about investments—oh, many things. Ah, well." She gave a preoccupied shrug and asked if the commander intended to stay to dinner.

Jim replied, "No, thank you. There are two policemen in the lobby. I think I'd better leave before they report my prolonged presence here."

Sue said, "But that doesn't matter now, Jim."

Pauline, however, spoke up sharply. "Oh, but it is important. It is sensible. In a court, at a trial—no, it would do harm to admit that you spent too much time here. No, madame, he is quite right." She tossed her jet-black head and departed.

"Jim, he ought to have left Jean more than a thousand dollars."

"Don't worry about Miss Wilson. I'm sure Pauline's right. She's also right about my staying here so long; I'd better leave. I'll phone later."

When he had gone she leaned back, looked at the sky and thought about Jean Wilson and about Jim and herself. A trial, Pauline had said with practical and frightening foresight. Presently it struck her again that the terrace was no longer a pleasant place. The sun had gone; the sky showed only a faint lemon-colored line toward the west. The shadows on the terrace were heavy and seemed to move. All her ideas about Marcus and Rose had been changed. Rose hadn't loved him and he hadn't loved her; yet they were wedded, linked not only in their lives but in their deaths.

She could no longer sit in the darkness of the haunted terrace. She went inside and after a while was summoned to dinner. Pauline was in a quiet, almost brooding state of mind, which Sue did not question, for she suspected that the maid was thinking about Rose.

Pauline brought the coffee tray upstairs. Everything was done with a kind of taut dignity, as if it was a time of emergency in which one tried to cling to everyday conventions. While Sue was having coffee, Woody was announced without benefit of the scribbled note pad and silver tray. "I knew that Madame would wish to see him," Pauline said. She was still in a morose mood, but her eyes had an odd glitter as she shoved up her black hair, said "Good night, madame," and scuttled into the small elevator. Sue hoped that Pauline was not about to have another *crise de nerfs*. Still, she couldn't really blame her for feeling tense; nobody could like working in a house where murder had struck twice.

As Woody came across the gallery he said, "Pauline opened the door and ran like a rabbit. Looks to me as if you'll have to get a new maid soon." He dropped down into a chair beside her and refused coffee. "Poor Sue. I heard all about today—Aubrey told me. Where's Jim Locke?"

"I haven't the least idea," she said truthfully.

"You should have taken my advice," Woody said. "It would be better if you saw nothing of him, for a while, at any rate. Now what about this window washer? I take it that he was the man who phoned you while I was here and asked about a reward."

"You heard him. You took the phone—"

"He didn't say anything. That is, just a jumble about money and a reward. Nothing that made any sense. What did he say when he came here to see you?"

"He said he saw Jim—that is, a man in a blue uniform—come out on the terrace and plant the flowers. Then Marcus appeared, they talked, and—and he saw Marcus fall. It's a dreadful story, but he must have invented it."

"Yes, of course. And Jim was wearing a uniform that day?"

"You saw him that morning. His clothes were too big, you see; he'd lost so much weight. He stopped in somewhere and ordered a couple of ready-made new suits, but since his uniform was new and it fit him, he wore that."

"Too bad. But Aubrey says that Conti seemed very reasonable about the whole thing. Of course, the police must be sure they have grounds for arresting Jim. They'll have to find the window washer, but that shouldn't be hard. Then Conti will have to check his story thoroughly before taking any drastic steps. It's clearly an attempt at blackmail, and that alone partially discredits the window washer. Not entirely, though."

"But he *couldn't* have seen Jim."

"Sue, are you *sure* that you're still in love with this young man?"

"I wish you wouldn't call him 'this young man.' His name—"

"Are you still in love with him? Or do you just *think*

you're still in love with him? I mean, is he really still the same man? You must remember that he's had some terrible experiences. I don't mean merely the concussion or his illness; I mean the long months of struggling for existence, about which we know nothing. We can't even guess how it might change a man."

"Jim hasn't changed."

Woody took out a cigarette, and the flare of the match accented his handsome, blunt profile, his blue eyes and firm mouth. "All right," he said at last, "all right. But if he did push Marcus over that wall, as the window washer says he did—"

"I know he didn't!"

"All I want to say is this: if Conti gets around to arresting him—really I should say *when* he arrests him, for I don't see how he can fail to—I'll do anything I can for you or for your Jim. Of course, when they do get hold of this window washer, he may break down completely and confess that he was only trying to get some money out of you—anything. He doesn't sound like a rational character. Aubrey says he was so drunk and abusive that it was impossible to control him. I wish I'd questioned him over the phone, but if he'd heard a man's voice, he might have shut up completely. Actually, he seemed so incoherent and wild that I never thought you'd hear from him again. But the fact is"—he rose and paced thoughtfully across the room and back—"the fact is that once the word murder has been uttered, then the police are bound to pursue the case until they've solved it."

"Woody, I really know so little about Rose and Marcus' life. They must have known many people I've never even heard of. Suppose some stranger—I mean stranger to me—had had a dreadful quarrel—"

Woody eyed her attentively. "Did Jean Wilson come up here this afternoon?"

"Yes. She said she had talked to you and Aubrey."

"I didn't think she'd come."

"So you knew about her. Did many people know?"

He smiled. "Good heavens, how should I know that? I've never heard it talked about."

"She said a queer thing. She said that Rose deserved to be murdered."

Woody's face went perfectly blank. "Jean said that?"

"And Pauline said that Rose knew all about Jean and Marcus and that she didn't care."

"I don't suppose she did care," Woody said slowly and turned toward the windows. He stood with his back to her for a long time before he said in a queerly muffled voice, "Rose had her own interests."

"Rose? I can't believe that Rose—" She stopped as he came back, sat down beside her on the sofa and took her hand. He held it lightly, looking at it, turning it over and over. "Call me anything you like, Sue. At best I was a besotted young fool. I was in love with Rose. I thought I couldn't live unless I saw her and talked to her and listened to her and—just watched her move and smile and . . . Well, there it was. But she was Marcus' wife. Rose knew how I felt, of course; she couldn't have helped knowing. So when she was killed, I—" He put her hand down gently. "I nearly died too. But of course I recovered—one does. I was always thankful, though, that Marcus never knew. But Jean may have guessed it. She has very sharp eyes."

"She didn't say anything about you . . . I'm sorry, Woody."

"Oh, I'm not the first man to make a fool of himself. It

was worse because of Marcus, of course; he'd done so much for me. But I've always had a notion that perhaps—just perhaps, that quality which made Rose so attractive may have had something to do with her murder."

Sue asked the obvious question. "You mean that a jealous woman killed her?"

"Or a jealous man. Did Marcus ever talk about her death to you?"

"He never talked about her at all. Except—oh, in a general way he might mention her when it would have been more painful to avoid her name than to say it. Woody, was there—do you think that Rose might have been in love with another man?"

He rose. "I'm sure that she didn't love Marcus."

"But suppose she was in love with another man, he—well, he wouldn't have killed her."

"It doesn't seem likely."

"If there was another man, who was he?"

"How should I know! She wouldn't have told me. Oh, Aubrey squired her around when Marcus wasn't at home—to the theatre, concerts, that kind of thing. And of course Aubrey does seem to be attractive to women."

She had an impulse to laugh. "Aubrey!"

"I know. I've never been able to see it myself. Besides, Aubrey enjoys being foot-loose and fancy free. He wouldn't have wanted to give that up. He could dine out every night if he wanted to."

"But Rose in *love* with him?"

"There's no use trying to explain what makes people tick. By the way, where's that book of Rose's that Marcus gave you? It had recipes and things in it."

"The day book? Pauline has it, I think."

"There were some entries, the last entry she made. We

were looking at it. It was there on the table, I think, the afternoon Marcus was up on the parapet."

"I looked at the book later. There are only menus and things like that."

"I suppose so, but it struck me that there just might be something to give us some kind of clue. Since this young man of yours has got himself in this ticklish position, we may have to rake up Rose's murder and try to find out who killed her. And if it links up with Marcus' death . . . There may be no link at all, of course, but I'd like to look through the book."

"All right, I'll ask Pauline for it, but I don't think it will help us."

"And Sue, remember what I told you: one does forget."

Somehow she did not think that he had forgotten.

On an impulse, she said, "Did it ever occur to you that Marcus might have killed Rose?"

Woody's face was blank again. "Certainly; I thought of everything. But I don't believe it. For one thing, he was too smart. For another, he really had what amounted to a firm alibi—"

The telephone rang at last; she knew that it must be Jim. Woody sensed it too, for he said, "I suppose I can't prevent your talking to him."

She ran to the telephone in her bedroom. Jim sounded cross and tired. "I got rid of the watchdogs for the moment, I think. How does that private elevator of yours work?"

"The door in the lobby locks automatically; it has to be opened from the inside unless you have the key. Are you coming back here? I'll go down and open it."

"Give me five minutes; I'm around the corner. I'll knock three times on the door of the elevator when I think the coast is clear."

When she came back to the living room Woody was smiling. "Well, at any rate he seems to be trying not to attract attention. If I were his lawyer and I thought there would be a trial, I'd try to make him stay away from here."

"I'm going down to the lobby."

"Yes, I heard. Go ahead."

She entered the little dimly lit cage and pressed the lobby button. Hopefully, Pauline's lynxlike ears would not hear the rumble as the elevator passed the dining-room floor. It glided smoothly down and down, stopping with a faint jolt. She waited for what seemed a long time, but actually it was only a matter of moments before Jim knocked lightly on the door. She pushed it open and he slid quickly into the cage, the door closing behind him. Laughing a little, he shrugged his coat straight and took a long breath as she started the elevator up again. "They were good men. Like hounds. I tried everything I could think of. All the stores were closed, so I couldn't duck in anywhere and lose myself. I tried Grand Central, but they hung on like glue. I jumped into a cab and then jumped out at a traffic light, but they stuck right to me. Finally I headed back here openly, so they thought that this was my destination and hung back a little. As soon as they did, I shot around the corner to a drugstore and phoned you."

"Where are they now?"

Jim laughed again. "I took them by surprise; they were pretty cocky by that time. They ran around to Madison and I came back the same way I'd gone. Polk was down at the corner whistling for a taxi; when I dashed into the lobby they were questioning him. I think he saw me out of the tail of his eye, so he kept pointing in the wrong direction. Anyway, I got here. Not that it really matters," he said, suddenly sober. "I just didn't want them to know that I'm going to stay here all night."

"You're going to—?"

"That wasn't any dream you had last night. I think somebody got into the apartment."

The elevator gave its decorous little lurch and stopped. Jim opened the door, saw Woody and said, "Oh—"

"Hello, Locke. Glad to see you. I'll make us some drinks and then make myself scarce," Woody said tactfully.

chapter 18

Woody left tactfully again perhaps an hour later. They had a drink, talked, smoked, had another drink and talked some more, but they settled nothing. Nothing could be done until the police had gleaned what they could from the window washer.

"I'll try to find Rose's book," Sue promised as Woody left.

"Probably nothing in it," he said.

"He was in love with Rose," Sue told Jim when he'd gone. She repeated everything she could remember that Woody had said. "He still loves her, you see—at least, he can't forget her."

"Rose seems to have been quite a girl," Jim said.

"She didn't look . . . I mean, she was always so beautiful and poised and cool."

"Made trouble all the same," Jim said thoughtfully.

"Maybe it was Woody himself who got tired of it and hit her over the head. Or Marcus. Or somebody else—somebody we don't know about. This lover of Rose's—if there was one. What is this book you were talking about?"

"A notebook that Rose kept for menus and household things."

"Not a diary?" Jim asked with a flicker of hope.

"No, nothing like that at all. When Woody saw it here, it happened to be open at the last entry. It was dated the day she died. He thought that she might have written something there that might give us a clue."

"Let's take a look at it."

"Pauline put it away. I'll get it in the morning. But I've looked the book through and there's nothing like evidence."

"What about the last page?"

"I didn't really read it after seeing the date. I think there were some directions to Pauline; her name was there. It was only a scribble which broke off. It was horrible. I thought it looked as if somebody had interrupted her."

"Perhaps someone did," Jim said soberly. "Well, now, nobody is going to try to get into the place tonight, but if there's anything at all, I'll hear it. Get me a blanket or something, will you?"

She got the eiderdown from her bedroom and a pillow. "Pauline will know you're here. I don't know what she'll think."

"You know perfectly well what she'll think. Don't be an ass. Good night." Yawning, he stretched out on the sofa.

Jim was gone before she awoke in the morning. She would scarcely have believed that he had been there if the pillow and eiderdown had not still been on the sofa, and an ashtray full of cigarette ends on the table. She pulled the curtains open and tidied up. Jim had obviously gone down by the private elevator very early, unseen, she hoped.

Still, if he were arrested and charged with murder, if there was a trial, there was not much use in trying to conceal anything. She went soberly down the stairs, opened the hall door to pick up the morning newspapers and walked back to the kitchen to speak to Pauline.

But Pauline was nowhere in the place. She had left a note, propped dramatically against the coffee pot. Its contents were theatrical too: "Madame: Il faut que je part. A trial c'est impossible. Je suis une domestique de good character et il faut que je protect the standing. Aussi je l'ai peur. Je comprend toutes les affaires. Adieu. Mes bagages sont pret a partir aussi. Pauline."

She read it again, disentangling the mixture of French and English: "Madame: It is necessary that I leave. A trial is impossible. I am a domestic of good character and it is necessary to protect my standing. Also I am afraid of it." (Did she mean the trial? Sue wondered.) "I understand all the affairs. Good-bye. My baggage is ready to leave also."

The practical concern about her baggage was typical of Pauline, as was her feeling that if she were involved in a trial, it would injure her chances of getting another good position. What was not at all typical was her fear of the spotlight if she was called as a witness.

But the departure was certainly final. Sue found Pauline's room was neat, her trunk locked and ready to go. There were several boxes and a suitcase, and the bed was made up with fresh linen. Rose's day book lay on the tidy bedside table. As she picked it up, another note from Pauline fell from it: "Dear Madame, I copy out recipes and some menus."

She would miss practical Pauline, Sue thought. Eventually, if there was a murder charge and a trial, the police would soon find her.

Standing there in Pauline's spotless room, she flipped through the day book again, but there were only menus, recipes, abbreviated scraps of memos. She doubted whether Woody could make anything of them; certainly if there had been anything which had the slightest connection with Rose's murder, Marcus himself would have seen it. Carrying the book, she went back to the kitchen and made coffee.

Upstairs again, she gathered up glasses and straightened the room. The penthouse began to seem very quiet. But the terrace was sunny, though the sky was rather hazy; the hedge was showing a firmer tinge of green, the geraniums were blooming happily and there were no shadows there.

It seemed remarkable that her images of Marcus and Rose had been so very different from their real selves. She felt as if she had been looking at portraits which, though fine in color and design, bore no resemblance to their subjects. She could almost see Rose's beautiful face, so calm, so sure of itself, so beautiful—and perhaps so deceptive.

She settled herself down again with the schoolgirlish, neat pages of Rose's book. At the end of an hour she had found no more than lists of names, initials, menus, recipes, charts for the seating of dinner parties, more menus, more recipes. It was nothing more than a book of housekeeping notes. She discovered that the secret of sauce for *duck à l'orange* was a dash of orange bitters and that Yorkshire pudding must be made with whole milk. Occasionally there were cryptic comments on a dinner party or a guest in Rose's own brand of abbreviated and mixed French and English, which resembled Pauline's.

Though it was undated, the book had apparently been kept over a period of years. The last page was no different from the others; there was a recipe for veal with sour cream and white wine, the address and telephone number of some caterers . . . But that wasn't the last page! The last page had been dated August 12th, Sue remembered, the day that Rose was murdered. She had seen only that date, together with Pauline's name and a scribble of handwriting before she had slammed the book shut in horror.

Now, as she looked closely, she saw that the page had been torn out; a tiny scrap of torn paper was caught in one of the rings of the notebook.

The doorbell rang and she ran to answer it. Belle hurried inside, closed the door sharply behind her and gave Sue a penetrating look. "Haven't you heard? Haven't they told you? Are the police here?"

"What? Belle, what?"

"I thought you must have been told by now. It's in the papers too. Both Woody and Aubrey phoned me. It's that window washer. They fished him out of the East River sometime last night."

After what seemed a long time, Sue said, "Was he murdered too?"

Belle nodded. Even at this moment she was carefully dressed in white gloves, another smart spring suit, pearls at her throat and in her ears, lipstick on her trembling mouth. Nevertheless, she looked her age and more. "Come upstairs. No need for Pauline to hear us."

"Pauline's gone."

"Where?" Belle asked sharply.

"I don't know. She left a note. She didn't want to appear as a witness at any trial. What are the police doing?"

Belle was preceding her up the stairs; one stocking seam, twisted along her slim leg, described, as perhaps nothing else could, her state of mind. She looked down at Sue around the curve of the stairs. "If you mean have they arrested Jim Locke, I don't know. But Aubrey says there's no doubt the window washer was murdered. His head"—Belle swallowed, turned away and marched upward—"his skull was smashed. It's in the papers."

Sue expected the story to be headlined with Marcus'

name and the mention of murder. But Belle turned to an inside page and pointed only to a small paragraph. The gist of it was that the body of a man had been recovered from the river by the police at about two in the morning. The time of his murder was not definitely established but was within an hour or two of the discovery. Apparently he had been the victim of a street thugging and robbery, for his wallet was gone. He had been identified, however, by his social security card pinned inside a coat pocket. His name was Antonio Napel.

"It's the same man," Belle said. "The police checked. He worked for a window-washing firm that sends men to buildings around this neighborhood. They've already asked the service-elevator man in this building if he ever saw the man. They took him down to the—the morgue. The man confirmed the fact that Napel had come here to your penthouse twice. The second time was yesterday and he was so drunk that the elevator man was worried. Did Jim Locke kill him?"

"No! No—"

"Where is Jim?"

"I don't know. I *really* don't know, Belle."

"The police will find him. For your sake, I hope he has an alibi."

He has an alibi, Sue thought with relief; he was here. Then she realized it was close to midnight when Jim had arrived. The police might claim that Jim had killed the window washer before coming up, or that he had sneaked out when she was asleep. In any case, they would doubt her word.

"Aubrey says they've got to arrest Jim now. Woody says they may merely hold him for questioning." Suddenly Belle's composure broke and she put her hands over her face. "You don't realize what it will be like! A murder investigation! Now they'll be sure that Marcus was murdered and that the window washer could identify Jim and that Jim killed him to prevent it—"

"Stop, Belle! He didn't!"

"I know how you feel, but look at the facts. This Napel was close enough to see a man in blue, and Jim was wearing his uniform that day. The window washer must have been near enough to see his face."

"Suppose Marcus' murder was linked to Rose's murder, Belle?"

"You mean that Jim didn't even know Rose? It's a strong argument in his favor, is that it? How do you know he didn't know her?"

"I know. Belle, I have to ask it, was there any man Rose . . . well, liked?"

Belle's eyelids fluttered; then she looked firmly at Sue. "Perhaps. Rose was very attractive. Very beautiful."

"So there was a man. Who?"

"You must believe me—Rose never talked to me about another man. But yes, there were times when I was sure Rose was in love with somebody. I didn't think she would divorce Marcus—he wouldn't have allowed it—but sometimes I did feel that she might just leave him. She was like that—impatient, self-willed, very self-confident. But I also had a queer notion that the man she was in love with didn't really love her. I don't know why, I can't explain. Small things. When you know somebody as well as I knew Rose, there are things you see, straws in the wind. Sometimes Rose was happy in that special glowing kind of way that you can't mistake, and yet I felt that she wasn't sure about the man. But whoever he was, nothing like that ever came out. It was a great relief to me. If Marcus knew, it must have been a relief to him too, though honestly I don't think he ever suspected. He had a life of his own, after all," she added dryly.

Sue wondered briefly if there was anything that Belle didn't know or intuit. Yes, there was one thing: she didn't know who had murdered Rose or Marcus.

"Yes, I know," she answered to Belle's last remark.

Belle gave her a swift look. "How did you know?"

"She came here yesterday. Jean Wilson."

"Oh. What did she want?"

"I think really to—to see me, talk to me. She was obviously very upset by Marcus' death."

"He should have left her more money," Belle said shortly. "It wouldn't have hurt him to set her up for life. I'll do something about that. But you can see that Rose had some justification. There was nothing I could do, Sue, nothing at all. Sometimes I felt as if I were watching people head straight for disaster, and yet I was helpless. Sometimes everything on the surface would be so pleasant and agreeable that I'd tell myself I was being a foolish old woman. But then Rose was murdered."

"Belle, if Rose—if there was a man who didn't reciprocate Rose's feelings, do you think they could have quarreled?"

"Because Rose wouldn't leave him alone? So he finally murdered her to get rid of her? It doesn't seem reasonable. Certainly there are easier ways to get rid of a woman. And remember, there was never any proof that there *was* a man. To tell you the truth, I wouldn't have wanted to find that kind of proof. I prefer to remember my daughter—I prefer people to remember my daughter as they knew her," Belle said steadily.

"You were right, dear Belle."

"Most men liked Rose. Woody was a constant escort. Of course, Rose was older. She wouldn't have been interested in somebody young who was not really settled in life. She had her pride and her—call it vanity. She liked to glitter, you know. She adored dinner parties, balls, that kind of thing. She didn't want Marcus to enter politics at all; she loathed the idea of officialdom. But he insisted; he said she would have to go back and campaign with him at election time, but by then—" Belle's lips shook a little and she quickly lowered her head—"by then of course, it was too late."

Sue said tentatively, "Could she have been in love with Aubrey?"

Belle gave her a startled glance. "Aubrey! Good heavens!" At any other time Sue felt she might have giggled at the thought but now her forehead wrinkled as she said, "Of course, Aubrey is attractive, and he was even more attractive six years ago, not so—proper. I've never liked him, though everybody else does. He's very popular. But then an unattached man in New York is invited everywhere. Of course," she said after a moment's pause, "I've learned one peculiar thing about life and love. Nobody can guess why a woman make a fool of herself over some perfectly ordinary man. Or, for that matter, why a man goes off the deep end over some utterly boring woman. Nothing can explain it; it's like flu or something—you just get it. Rose may have gone out of her head about somebody, but I don't know who."

Belle left a few minutes later. There was nothing they could do, she pointed out, until the police made some sort of move. "And they'll make it," she said at the door downstairs, leaning forward to kiss Sue. "Let me know if you hear anything."

Back in the living room, Sue absently took up Rose's book again. Possibly Pauline had removed the last page; certainly someone had torn it out. Only its removal suggested some significance, though there might merely have been a recipe which Pauline wished to take with her. But Sue's thoughts seemed to run along two tracks, and only one had anything to do with Rose's day book. She remembered that Marcus had retrieved it from the kitchen or pantry and handed it to her; then Woody had seen it and they had both remarked on the date on the last page and the possibility that Rose might have been horribly interrupted. Sue had hurriedly put it away when Marcus arrived; later that night she had got it out again before Jim came back. She had been looking at the book when the house telephone rang, and she had left it on the table then. It must have stayed there until the next day, when Senator Stidger and Aubrey had come to call. Then Marcus had come in and there had nearly been a fight, and Aubrey had knocked the book to the floor. Later Belle had picked it up and talked about Rose. But Aubrey, Woody, Belle, Senator Stidger, Marcus and even Jim had all had an opportunity at least to see the book. Pauline had asked for it and at last obviously had taken it away.

Sue put the book away in a drawer of the table and began to concentrate on her other preoccupation, which was more urgent. What were Jim and the police doing?

During the afternoon she read Pauline's farewell note again. It puzzled her; there was something almost knowing and secretive about it. "I understand all the affairs"; *affaires* in French could mean "everything," or perhaps it only referred to Pauline's efficiency in household matters. "I am afraid of it" could mean the trial and its possible effect on Pauline's professional standing—or it could mean that she was afraid of what they might force her to reveal.

In the end, because she knew Pauline's love of drama and her capacity for histrionics, Sue discounted any hidden meanings. In any event, she had no idea where the woman had gone; if there were more to the note than appeared, then the police would have to find her and wrest the meaning from her.

This was not a very satisfactory conclusion, for in a curious way Pauline's presence seemed to remain. Sue kept imagining she could hear her whisking skirts and the small rattle and clatter from the kitchen. But the day crept on and nothing happened except that a gray cloud layer appeared and hovered heavily all at once over the terrace and its bright pink flowers. It was so quiet in the penthouse that she began to feel as if she were cut off from everything in the world. She smoked too much; she listened; she waited; she drank too much coffee; she waited.

At about six o'clock rain began to patter dismally down upon the terrace. She turned on lights and went slowly downstairs again to make more coffee. When she returned to the living room to pace the floor, the emptiness and isolation of the apartment seemed to creep more closely and tenaciously around her. She felt she couldn't escape something that made no sound and had no presence, but *something* was there, waiting as she was waiting. She didn't dare go for a walk in the rain, as she longed to do to exorcise the phantoms that crowded around; she was sure that if she left the place, Jim would come or someone would telephone, and that she would miss something important. *Wait,* she told herself for the hundredth time that afternoon. Nothing could have been harder.

At last Aubrey telephoned. He and Woody were at Belle's apartment. Conti had arrested Jim, and bail had been set at a hundred thousand dollars. Woody and Aubrey and Belle were getting together the money.

"Where is he?" Sue asked.

"In the Tombs. He was arraigned in double-quick time—" Aubrey checked himself as Woody's voice sounded in the background. "Woody says you'd better come here and stay with Belle. I think so too."

She didn't hesitate for a second; she would go anywhere to escape the haunted penthouse. "Yes, yes, I will. But I want to see Jim. When will they release him?"

"As soon as we arrange bail, I think. We'll hurry."

"Bring him to Belle's."

"Yes, yes—"

Now Woody came on the phone. "Sue, it's going to be all right. They won't convict him. Don't worry."

"Of course, yes. It'll be all right. They won't convict him," she said like a parrot, not believing it. "Oh, Woody, I found Rose's book, and the last page—"

Belle's voice cut in then as she took the telephone from Woody. "Hurry up, Sue, the traffic is already snarled up by the rain. I'll expect you." She hung up.

But Sue didn't hurry. She *tried* to hurry, but she was clumsy and forgetful and slow. Jim's arrest meant that the police believed he had murdered the window washer, and thus that he had killed Marcus. But if the same person had killed Marcus and Rose, they must realize that it couldn't be Jim. Surely Conti could find no link between Rose and Jim; none existed. But they were investigating Marcus' murder now, not Rose's. The Tombs was a massive gray building far downtown. It would take Woody and Aubrey a long time to make their way there through the wet dusk and the heavy traffic. Then there would be all the formalities to get Jim out.

A trial, a defense, a jury. But Jim had nothing to do with Rose's murder, and that was a strong argument, as Belle had said. Yet she had often heard that nobody can ever tell what a jury will do.

In trying to hurry, she dropped her slippers. She gathered up her toilet articles and half of them slid out of her hands. She pulled out a lingerie drawer with a jerk that spilled everything on the floor. For a long while she couldn't find her suitcase, and finally discovered it exactly where it should be. It was later than she had thought. Traffic must already be heavy; even twelve stories up she could hear the whistles of doormen and the horns of angry taxis. But she knew in her bones that she was never coming back to live in this haunted apartment, so she made herself take the time to gather what she needed until somebody could come and pack whatever else belonged to her. In truth, there was very little. She remembered to snatch up her father's picture along with brushes, comb, lipsticks and toothbrush. Oh, I can buy these, she thought impatiently, and yet she kept picking up oddments and throwing them in her suitcase. Then she couldn't get it closed; somehow she had jammed the lock.

Jim was in the Tombs. At last she got the suitcase closed. She put on a raincoat over her yellow sweater and skirt and then thought dimly that she ought to change into something more suitable. A semblance of common sense returned; she thought, Suitable for what? She picked up the suitcase and was at the door of the living room when she remembered the box holding Jim's ring. She had to take that with her. She went to the drawer and had pulled everything out of it and out of every other drawer before she remembered that she had not put the box away the previous night. Jim had looked at it, then closed it and put it down on a table in the living room.

She hurried back to the living room, but the box was not on the table. Though she searched thoroughly, it was nowhere in the room.

It began to seem hours since she had talked to Belle and Aubrey and Woody. She glanced out toward the terrace, now dark, with rain streaking the black windows, and then drew the green curtains. Again she searched for the candy box, but finally she had to accept the fact that it had disappeared again. She must leave without it.

She had forgotten her handbag. She turned back to the bedroom, and stumbled over the suitcase at the end of the sofa. She wondered why she had been such a fool as to pack anything at all. It would be almost impossible to get a taxi now. Well, she could walk to Belle's apartment; it was not far. She must leave *now;* in the back of her mind there was an urgent notion that she must *hurry*. The little French clock struck briskly seven times. The melodious, familiar chimes echoed in the empty apartment. She then heard another familiar sound. It was the unmistakable little rumble and hum of the private elevator, and it was coming nearer.

chapter 19

The elevator purred closer. Sue's first thought was that Pauline had returned. Possibly Aubrey had a key too; certainly she was not afraid of him. However, somebody was coming; in another second or two the rumble would stop, the elevator would give its quiet little lurch and the door would open.

Then she remembered something so trivial that she had never given it another thought: the shriveled brown geranium leaf she had found in the cage a few days before. At the time she remembered thinking idly that Pauline had not dusted. She then knew who had murdered Rose and Marcus, and who was in the elevator.

A whole series of obscure signs on a dark road had suddenly been illuminated and leaped into terrifying significance.

Before the elevator could stop and the door opened, she did exactly what Rose had done. She ran for the gallery door, closed it softly behind her—and then stood frozen, realizing what she had done. Now there was no retreat. But perhaps the instinct of the hunted had told her that she couldn't have escaped by way of the stairs or the back door. The person in the elevator could run faster and might have a gun. The roar of the traffic surged up from the street, and she could hear nothing from the penthouse. But she had only to unlock the wrought-iron gate, feel her way across the roof through the rain to the lighted back stairway and descend very cautiously, but very quickly.

Again she failed—exactly as Rose must have failed: she couldn't unlock the gate. She fumbled desperately through her handbag for her key ring. Her hands were cold and unsteady, but she found the key ring. In the faint glow in the sky from millions of lights reflecting themselves rosily against the low clouds, she found the padlock. She tried one key after another, and then tried them all over again, but she didn't have the key for the gate. She had a faint recollection of its hanging on a hook in the gallery or in the pantry; perhaps she had never really known where it was kept. She tried all her keys over again, even knowing that none of them would fit. She pushed and pulled the lock. Nothing would open it.

Perhaps she should have tried to go downstairs and ring for the regular elevator. But there would have been the sound of her running feet on the stairs, the sound of the hall door opening and closing, the dangerous wait until the elevator man noted her signal and came up to the eleventh floor—if he were not obliged to wait for somebody in the lobby or to stop at intervening floors. Murder could be done very quickly.

Murder? The instant she had heard the hum of the elevator she had known that her own murder was intended. It couldn't be real.

But she was safe! The apartment looked empty; in it was only the murderer, searching. Then she remembered with clammy horror that proof of her presence, her suitcase, was still in the living room. It would prove that she was there, somewhere.

Perhaps it would not be seen. She tried to think just where she had left it—the end of the sofa? The sofa would hide it, wouldn't it?

A thin line of light from the drawn curtains of the gallery fell across the terrace at her feet. The only light on the terrace, it reached almost to the corner where Rose had been murdered and where she now huddled. For an instant the light disappeared, as if someone was blocking the gallery door and was about to open it, but then it reappeared. It seemed likely that the whole penthouse was being searched. Of course her suitcase would be discovered if it had not already been seen, and searched as it had been earlier. Now she knew why: since the likeliest places in the penthouse had been combed over unsuccessfully while she was staying at Belle's, the obvious conclusion was that the evidence of murder had been in her suitcase and was still there.

It would be almost impossible now for the guilty person to believe that she had no real evidence. It was dangerous evidence which she could not be permitted to tell. It seemed cruelly ironic that in fact she still did not know exactly what the evidence was, but she realized that she knew too much. Again she shook the wrought-iron gate; again it was wet and cold and immovable. In the normal world, twelve stories below, traffic hooted and rumbled.

All right, she thought, I'll get away; I know how. She began to push the box of privet at the entrance of the fire escape. It was cold and wet and heavier than she had expected but she managed to shove it cautiously, terrified at the scraping sound. On the terrace the traffic sounded loud, but someone inside the penthouse might hear the scraping of the box across the tiles. But she persisted until she could squeeze between the box and the corner of the parapet; then she took a long breath and groped for the railing of the fire escape.

It was an open fire escape, terrifying now, for below there was only blackness except for an occasional shaft of misty light coming from some window. Away below she saw a street light, dim at that distance, haloed by streaks of rain. As she started down a doorman somewhere whistled for a taxi, and the sound shrilled weirdly over and over again through the drone of traffic and the rain and darkness. She clung to the wet, cold railing and felt her way carefully. She went down and down, one step at a time, clinging to the railing, feeling for each rung.

A few more steps and she would reach the dining-room windows. Perhaps one of them was not locked and she could slide it silently open, go very softly through the dining room, and out the back door to the service elevator. There might be a long wait for the operator, but she decided to try it.

Another step. Her hand on the railing felt slippery and awkward. Another—she stopped. Along the railing there was a slight vibration.

She waited a second or two and the vibration came again, the faintest trembling along the fire escape, communicating itself dreadfully to her own hand. Someone else was coming down from the terrace.

She had reached the tiny landing at the dining-room window; here the fire escape doubled back in a turn. She clutched at a window and pushed; it wouldn't open. She crossed the small open landing and tried the other window, desperately shoving upward with her fingers.

The casing below the lock yielded a little. She couldn't believe it, but there was no time to think. Sliding the window up, she tumbled over the still and into the room. Then she closed and locked the window behind her.

She was gasping for breath, she was hot and cold as she ran across the dark room, bumping into the table, careening away from it in the darkness, groping her way toward the pantry. But as she found the swinging door there was a clatter in the kitchen. It sounded as if someone had knocked over a chair.

Had her panic deceived her? Had she only fancied the pursuing tremor of the railing? There had been no one on the fire escape; her pursuer was in the kitchen instead.

But there was another refuge: the private elevator. The pantry was a long, narrow room, and it was unlikely that anybody in the kitchen could hear the elevator's hum as it came down from the living room. Its journey would take only a moment, and then she would be safe.

She groped along the wall, found the elevator button and pushed it hard. There was a tiny jolt from above, and instantly the elevator murmured softly and reassuringly. There was no sound from the kitchen; in another second or two she would be safe.

As the elevator reached the dining-room floor, she flung the door open and hurled herself into the cage. Too late she realized that the little space was pitch-black; the two lights which always shone in the elevator had been turned off.

The door had closed behind her, and the elevator shook itself faintly and started downward. She was not alone in the cramped black space.

Someone was breathing heavily beside her.

She cried desperately, "You can't hurt me! You can't touch me! You don't dare! It's only a minute or two before we reach the lobby floor. You can't possibly get away."

There was a pause and then a conversational reply, except that the voice was husky and breathless. "That was a narrow squeak. I thought you'd got away when you crawled in the dining-room window. I thought you went out the back door."

"What do you want?"

"Rose's day book, of course."

"It's up there, in the drawer of the table."

"I know. I found it. I want that last page. You tore it out. Give it to me."

"I haven't got it."

"You're afraid. Why? What have I done to you?"

"I'm *not* afraid."

"You think I killed her. Why?"

"No—no—"

"Yes, you do. Tell me why you think I killed her." From out of the blackness hands caught her hard by the throat. She couldn't breathe. Lights whirled before her eyes. She struggled and pushed, but the hands only gripped harder. She made some sort of strangling sound and the hands released her, but she knew they still hovered near her neck. "Ready to talk now? *Why?*"

"The—the geranium leaf. When I found it here I knew that whoever had killed Marcus must have a key to this elevator. The geranium leaf must have caught on your sleeve or coat and then dropped here. You came down in this elevator after planting the flowers and killing Marcus. That means there was an extra key. Rose's murderer must have had a key too. She had it made for you—she must have given it to you—"

"But there's no proof! It could have been anyone! What else do you think you know?"

"I don't know anything! I don't!"

The hands gripped her again, shutting off her breath. "No, no," she tried to say, and the hands relaxed a little.

"All right, what else?"

She drew in air, and life came back. But she had to talk to gain a few precious moments. "You—you saw Jim in his blue uniform. That was the only day he wore it. Marcus must have looked at Rose's day book that afternoon while I was gone. He must have seen the last page." She couldn't go on; yet she had to continue, for she could feel the hot nearness of those hands. She had just learned horribly that she would do almost anything for a mere breath of precious air—besides, the elevator would arrive at the lobby floor in a few more seconds. She faltered, but went on talking. "He must have guessed that you killed her. Then he phoned you; he'd have tried to get the whole story before telling the police or anyone else. But he'd have—" She mustn't say any more, but if she didn't talk she'd be choked to death then and there.

"Go on. *Go on!*"

"He'd have turned you in," she whispered. "Somehow you got hold of a blue uniform, and you came up in this elevator, using the key Rose had given you. Then you went out on the terrace and planted the flowers, I don't know why—"

There was a curious sound of amusement. "That fooled you all, didn't it? It was too simple for the police to see. I had to make it look as though Marcus had been planting the flowers, tying up the tree. It had to look as if *he* had been working out there. I tied the tree up; I was doing it when he came out and saw me."

"The window washer saw you. He could have identified

you. They'd have made him try to identify Jim, but he wouldn't have been able to; he'd never seen Jim at all. But he wouldn't have given up. He'd have kept nosing around until he found you and blackmailed you."

Her raincoat was hideously hot. The elevator must reach the lobby floor in a few more seconds. She mustn't talk, but she had to talk to continue breathing.

"Go on, go on. What else?"

"But you didn't take Rose's book!"

"No, I . . . that was a mistake. I wasn't . . . myself. I hurried. I was in the street when I remembered that book! I couldn't go back to look for it then . . . You said I killed Rose."

Again she could feel the hands on her throat ready to close. "No, no, don't! I'll talk . . . you killed Rose because she wouldn't let you break it off. You couldn't go on with her, and—"

"Give me that last page."

"I don't have it!"

"You must have it."

"No, no. You must believe me! You took the box with my letters from Jim and it wasn't there!"

"Yes, and I returned the box. Now give me that last page!'

"I haven't got it—" Her handbag was wrenched away from her as the elevator stopped. She pushed as hard as she could against the door, but it wouldn't open. Suddenly she realized that the elevator wasn't at the lobby floor at all.

Hands caught at her throat again and she pulled at them, tearing at them with her fingernails, gasping, "It's stopped! It's stopped between floors!"

"What's happened?"

"I don't know."

The hands let her go, but they were still there in the stifling closeness of the little cage. She felt a movement at the panel of buttons controlling the elevator. One of them, she knew, was an alarm; if that was pressed, somebody would hear and come to her rescue.

The hope was instantly destroyed. "Which is the alarm button? I'll have to take the risk of the alarm. No, then somebody will come— What's *that*?"

Now the elevator was slowly rising. Someone had done something to its mechanism. She didn't know why or how; she was only conscious that beside her in the darkness there stood a murderer—Rose's murderer, Marcus' murderer, the murderer of a shabby little man who had nerved himself with Dutch courage before returning to threaten her for the last time.

She knew that in the tiny confines of that black cage the killer was debating his choices. She had to be killed too; that was clear. She knew or had guessed too much, and it had been choked out of her. She ought to have lied, invented, refused to talk—but nobody can do that when breath and life is relentlessly being squeezed away. Would she be strangled now, her breath cut off forever, plummeting into whirling darkness, left in the elevator until she was found? That was one choice for the killer; the other was that it might be wiser to kill her in the penthouse and throw her over the parapet. So easy. It was more likely that this choice would be adopted; it would be safer, for it might be ruled as suicide because of grief over Marcus' death.

All at once a sound like a sob and a moan came from the darkness close to her. "I didn't mean it to be like that! I wanted her influence with Marcus. Marcus was important to me. Things went too far. I tried to put a stop to it. She threatened me that last day; she said she'd tell Marcus. There was nothing else for me to do—I had to!"

Then the door was flung open and she fell backward into the living room against a chair. She caught a swift glimpse of Pauline's black eyes staring from a white face. There was a shout, a figure thrust past her, running for the terrace; there was a thud and Conti went sprawling. Then he jumped up again, and ran after the figure onto the terrace. Pauline was screaming, and old Duffy came waddling out from the gallery like a frightened duck. "I got the switch turned off in time," he panted. "We reversed the elevator. What are they doing out there on the terrace?"

Then Duffy had disappeared and Jim came running from the gallery. "He's going down the fire escape. I've got to phone—"

Pauline started for the bedroom, but Jim was ahead of her. In a minute she could hear him shouting, "Operator, this is an emergency. Police—" Seconds later he was running back through the living room. He gave Sue a swift look, knew that she was safe and ran back to the terrace.

The doorbell rang and Pauline hurried to answer it.

Sue was still huddled on the floor against the chair. Her raincoat was sickeningly hot; she struggled out of it and pulled herself up into the chair.

Belle entered, chattering to Pauline. "But he said that he was going to the Tombs. He said he was going to see about bail for Jim. What *happened*, Pauline? Why did you phone me? Why did you tell us to come here?"

"They found me," Pauline said. "They told me to phone you. Mr. Locke, he will tell you—"

Jim returned, breathing hard. "I got down three flights. They're way ahead of me. But the police will be at the bottom. They'll get him."

"Get who?" Aubrey said, appearing from the gallery. "Why did Pauline get me over here? What's going on? Get *who*?"

"Woody. He killed Marcus," Jim said. "And Rose. And the window washer."

It seemed to Sue that everybody was talking at once; their words shot out like rockets. Listening, she heard Jim say that when he had read Pauline's note that morning he too had thought it implied some suspicion or even actual knowledge. So he had copied it and taken it to Conti. The police were already looking for him and had arrested him when he walked into Conti's office. But Conti had initiated a search for Pauline; she had been comfortably checked in at a quiet hotel when she was found that afternoon, and at last she had talked. In the meantime, bail had been set. "Woody said that he would come to the Tombs to see about bail for me," Jim said. "But Conti felt sure that he'd come back here to find the book Pauline told us about. We—Pauline and Conti and I—came in the back way. Conti wanted to surprise Woody on the spot, with the book in his hands. But I knocked over a kitchen chair. Then we heard the elevator, and at first we thought that Sue must be taking it down from the top floor. But when we raced upstairs Woody was gone, so we figured he must be in there with her. So Conti rang through on the house phone to Duffy and told him to stop the cage until we could get some men at the lobby floor. But Duffy turned off the main switch and then he reversed the elevator and brought it back up here."

Belle clutched her hands together. "So it was Woody. I knew Rose had quarreled with somebody. Poor Rose—she couldn't give up, you see. It wasn't in her nature. But Woody was ambitious. Marcus would have ruined him."

Pauline moved over, took Belle's hand and said coolly, "I knew about that. Madame gave me five hundred dollars to help her."

So that was where that money had gone, Sue thought. Aubrey stared, "To help her do what?"

Pauline lifted her black head. "To run away with him, of

course. She had to tell me. She wanted to arrange a few things. Then that afternoon she sent me to the cinema. When I said good-bye she told me she would leave the housekeeping book for me so that I could use the recipes in my new place. Very choice recipes," she added matter-of-factly.

Agitatedly, Aubrey pulled out one of his enormous snowy handkerchiefs.

"And so," Pauline continued calmly, "I came home. I—well, I found what had happened. I didn't know, you understand, who had killed her. But naturally! How could one *know*! I phoned you, madame"—she looked at Belle—"and for the police, and to Mr. Desart's office. I can do nothing more. I keep the housekeeping book for myself. I say nothing about the five hundred dollars; I say nothing about Madame's intention to leave. Why should I hurt Mr. Desart and my friend Madame Minot! Or myself for knowing about Madame's plan and not telling her husband? *Ma foi*, I would never have got a good reference then!"

"Wait a minute," Aubrey said loudly, "do you mean to sit there and tell us that you knew Woody had killed Rose and you never told anybody?"

Pauline looked shocked. "No! No, no, no! I couldn't even suggest such a dreadful thing! Never! I only knew that she wished to go away with him. I—well, I guessed that he was not in agreement. He was afraid, but my madame was strong-willed. Perhaps there was a violent scene. I—I did know that a heavy tool, a fireplace tool, had disappeared. I replaced that later. I couldn't match it with the others, but nobody noticed."

I saw it, Sue thought; it meant nothing to me.

Pauline turned to Belle. "I'm sorry, madame. I did my best to—to protect everyone. And of course I have my old age to consider," she said blandly.

"Your—" Aubrey sputtered. "Why, you mean you expected to blackmail him into supporting you!"

Pauline lifted her eyebrows. "What a terrible idea! Of course, if he wished to give me little presents . . ." She shrugged. "And you must remember that I saw Mr. Woodard save Mr. Desart's life. How could I believe that the next day he killed him! No, no, never . . . Yet I began to think about that last page, and"—here she stopped, then said flatly—"I was scared. I wasn't sure, so . . . I left and took the page with me."

Belle spoke in a whisper. "The page?"

Sue explained. "The last page in Rose's day book. It began with Pauline's name. I started to read it, then I—oh, I didn't want to, because it was the last entry, made on the day she died. I remember, because no other entry was dated. Woody saw it too. It happened to be open, right there on the table, at that last page. He couldn't take it then because Marcus came in just at that moment. Later I took it away. But it was that afternoon when—" she swallowed hard—"Marcus himself suggested a way for Woody to kill him by getting dizzy on the parapet. Woody saved him then."

Jim said, "Conti thought—I did too—that Marcus may have discovered some new evidence. I remembered Woody asking you for the book and your telling him that you'd try to find it. Conti thinks that Marcus read that last page the day he was killed—probably after you went out for that long walk, Sue. Then he must have phoned Woody and told him to come over right away. Woody must have guessed from Marcus' tone that he knew the truth. Only Marcus' death could save him. He had his practice and his ambition to consider, and he had the terrible, unreasoning fear of a man who has once murdered. He remembered the incident of Marcus on the parapet the previous day, and he remembered seeing me in uniform—for all he knew, I always wore my uniform. He also knew I could be said to have a motive for murder, so he rented a doorman's uniform from a costume company. The police ran that down too, and his description. He changed right at the costume place, and put his own clothes in the box he carried. He was our stranger in blue. He had a key for the private elevator—"

Pauline said matter of factly, "But naturally. She gave it to him. A mistake, but—" She sighed.

"Conti thinks that when Woody arrived, Marcus must have been down in his study. Woody went out on the terrace; he had to coax Marcus out there. He waited—"

Sue said, "He planted the flowers, and after he killed Marcus he was beside himself, in a panic. He forgot to look for the book. He said—" All at once she found she could talk instead of just listen. Everything Woody had said in the blackness of the little elevator poured out. "But for a while—until it became too dangerous—he *was* in love with Rose; he told me so. Of course, he only admitted it because he thought Jean Wilson had already told me, and that if he brought it up himself, it would clear him of suspicion in my mind. And it did. But he couldn't have pretended so—so well, if he hadn't been in love with her once. And he really felt guilty and ashamed when he discovered that Marcus had left him money." For a moment she almost felt sorry for Woody, until she remembered the murderous strength in his hands.

There was a pause and then Jim said, "I took the candy box to Conti this morning, too. Woody's fingerprints were on it. Obviously he must have taken it while you were at Mrs. Minot's, found nothing in it and returned it the night he came up here. He thought that you had Rose's book in your suitcase, so he searched for it there. He must have hated to murder. He must have been in wild terror, too, running away without Rose's book . . ." He stopped suddenly, listened and said, "It's taking them a long time."

But it would take a long time to descend twelve flights of slippery, dark fire escape, far longer than it would take a man to fall from the parapet.

Suddenly, far below, a car honked wildly. Then others joined in. Brakes squealed, and Jim ran out to the terrace.

Aubrey looked at Pauline and said sternly, "You are an accessory after the fact—"

"Oh no," Pauline said airily. "I don't really *know* a single thing. Besides, I have been a great help to the police. A heroine, really," she said smugly.

Aubrey let out an angry breath. "You're an immoral woman," he shouted, and ran out to the terrace too. For a second Pauline looked almost flattered; then she followed him. Belle and Sue went out too and joined the others leaning over the hedge. Far below in the cross street they could see lights and hear horns. Voices but no words floated upward. From the end of the terrace, Aubrey shouted, "There's a crowd. Something's happened—"

Belle put her arm around Sue. "Let's go back inside."

For a long while they sat there, Belle smoking and thinking, both of them listening. Finally Jim and Aubrey came back in, both looking pale; and Pauline too, shuddering under her black coat. Aubrey poured some whiskey and gulped it down as Lieutenant Conti came across the gallery and into the living room. Nobody needed to ask anything; they knew.

At last Belle said to Lieutenant Conti, "I understand that tonight when Sue talked to Woody on the phone, she told him that she had found Rose's day book. He told me and Aubrey that he would go to the Tombs and arrange about

Jim's bail, but instead he came here. I don't understand why that last page was valuable to Pauline."

Pauline lifted her eyebrows and shrugged a little.

"I'll show it to you." Conti took a folded piece of paper from his pocket. "It's all right; it's only a photostat. But there it is—a little nest egg for . . . Well, never mind." He rubbed his red hair reflectively, glancing at Pauline. "It's odd how things work out. Pauline left that last page in the book for nearly six years, never thinking much about it. She need a recipe for a dessert and was in the kitchen with the book open when Mr. Desart simply walked in, said he wanted the book and took it away. Then she couldn't find it. She said that you"—he looked at Sue—"had put it away somewhere. By the time she did find it, Mr. Desart had died, so Pauline began to think. She went through the book and found—well, here it is." He waved the photostat of a ruled page torn at the edges.

The date was as Sue remembered it, August twelfth, and the message in Rose's and Pauline's shorthand mixture of French and English read: "Here is yr. bk. This is the day. He still thks unwise but I intend to go thru with it. Snd clos add. later kp. qut. for now about l'avocat, il arrive main—"

Conti said, "Pauline read it for us. It means: 'Here is your book. This is the day'—presumably the day Rose intended to leave. 'He still thinks it is unwise but I intend to go through with it. Send my clothes to the address I'll give you later. Keep quiet about the lawyer'—meaning Woody—'for now. He is arriving—' Pauline says that Rose meant to write 'maintenant,' meaning 'now.' "

For a while they sat silently. At last Conti said, "It's over, you know. He ran in front of a taxi. It was slippery. The driver couldn't stop."

After a moment Belle rose and came to Sue. "Stay with me if you want to—or—" She looked at Jim, stopped, kissed Sue a loving farewell and turned to Aubrey, who sprang forward and offered his arm. Pauline scurried after them. Unexpectedly Conti came over to Sue too and shook hands. "You're really all right now. I have everything I need, I think. Good wishes." Then he too walked away across the gallery and down the stairs, his footsteps sounding slow and tired.

The penthouse was silent again, but now it was a different silence. "You're alive," Sue said suddenly. "It didn't seem real—I couldn't really let myself believe—"

Jim pulled her into his arms. "There's a night plane we can get. I'm being sent to San Diego. Nobody out there will know anything about—anything. We can get married—"

No one except Jim was important. But she said, "Belle? Conti?"

"Oh, they knew. They understood. We can't be separated again—ever." He helped her on with her raincoat and picked up the suitcase which still stood at the end of the sofa.

For some reason they began to hurry down the gallery; for some reason they ran down the stairs. Behind them rain pattered softly on the terrace, on a shadow which had never really existed, on broken twigs which were already healing, growing small green leaves that were waiting for the summer sun.

About the author

Mignon Eberhart's name has become a guarantee of excellence in the mystery and suspense field. Her work has been translated into sixteen different languages, and has been serialized in many magazines and adapted for radio, television and motion pictures.

For many years Mrs. Eberhart traveled extensively, abroad and in the United States, with her husband, an engineer. Now they live in Westport, Connecticut, where she is a member of the Guiding Faculty of the Famous Writers' School. *Woman on the Roof* is her forty-fourth book.

